# In Rocco's world, no one summoned him, so it intrigued him to be at Clare's beck and call.

She was comfortable in her villa. She felt safe here. He wondered, though, what it would be like to have her feel a little less controlled, a little bit out of control, her mind and body overwhelmed by pleasure.

"Thank you for not keeping me waiting," she said crisply.

"Please." He sat, trying not to feel like a schoolboy called before the headmistress.

"You've spent your life devoted to your family, and you were an exceptional brother to Marius. He would be so happy you're here now, spending time with Adriano. He doesn't have a father, and I don't want to deprive him of anything—"

"So don't. Give him a father."

"And where do I find such a man?"

"You could marry me."

Clare's lavender eyes grew huge, her lips parting in shock. "But...you don't want to be married. You've made that abundantly clear."

"I don't wish to date, and I don't wish to start over. But you're not a stranger, and you have a son that needs a father, that could benefit from a family. From me."

*New York Times* and *USA TODAY* bestselling author **Jane Porter** has written forty romances and eleven women's fiction novels since her first sale to Harlequin in 2000. A five-time RITA® Award finalist, Jane is known for her passionate, emotional and sensual novels, and loves nothing more than alpha heroes, exotic locations and happily-ever-afters. Today Jane lives in sunny San Clemente, California, with her surfer husband and three sons. Visit janeporter.com.

### Books by Jane Porter

### Harlequin Presents

*The Prince's Scandalous Wedding Vow*
*Christmas Contract for His Cinderella*
*The Price of a Dangerous Passion*

### *Conveniently Wed!*

*His Merciless Marriage Bargain*

### *Passion in Paradise*

*His Shock Marriage in Greece*

### *Stolen Brides*

*Kidnapped for His Royal Duty*

Visit the Author Profile page
at Harlequin.com for more titles.

# *Jane Porter*

---

## THE CONVENIENT COSENTINO WIFE

Recycling programs for this product may not exist in your area.

ISBN-13: 978-1-335-59309-2

The Convenient Cosentino Wife

Copyright © 2023 by Jane Porter

For questions and comments about the quality of this book, please contact us at CustomerService@Harlequin.com.

Harlequin Enterprises ULC
22 Adelaide St. West, 41st Floor
Toronto, Ontario M5H 4E3, Canada
www.Harlequin.com

Printed in U.S.A.

# THE CONVENIENT COSENTINO WIFE

# PROLOGUE

THE FUNERAL WAS held the same weekend the wedding had been supposed to take place, although Rocco scheduled the private burial service for the day after the wedding, so as not to draw too many comparisons.

The funeral was very small as Rocco Cosentino wasn't interested in a drama-filled service for Marius, his younger brother, and only member of his family. Marius had been everything. His world, his responsibility, his hopes, his dreams. But then daring, fun-loving, bighearted Marius died after being thrown from a horse, doing what Marius loved—and knew—best. Polo had been Marius's passion, and so Rocco grieved, but it was his private grief, and he refused to have others there to witness his pain and loss. He'd raised his brother since Marius was six, and now Marius was gone.

Unfathomable. The aristocratic Cosentino bloodline ended with Rocco then, as Rocco would never marry, not again.

Rocco had politely, but firmly, told all that it was a private funeral, only family would be in attendance. But Rocco couldn't refuse Clare Redmond's attendance as the twenty-four-year-old American had been Marius's fiancée.

If Marius hadn't broken his neck, Clare would have been Marius's wife by now.

One could say, if only Marius hadn't played that final match on Wednesday, Clare would have been his sister-in-law, but it was too late for that. Accidents happened, and a most tragic accident had happened, and Marius, the little boy who'd become a brilliant, generous man, was forever gone.

Rocco stood next to the young American woman who'd arrived for the service shrouded in black, head to toe, wearing even a veil as if she'd stepped from a Gothic novel. He couldn't see her face, but he didn't need to—he could hear her weeping during the brief service, making Rocco wish the service was over.

It was said that funerals were for the living, not the dead, but Rocco had attended far too many in his life, and never once had he been glad to be there. Never once, had he thought ah, thank goodness for this archaic service filled with prayers and scripture that mean nothing to me. He'd never found comfort in the priest's words, not when he'd stood in the family plot for his father's funeral, his mother's funeral, his young bride's funeral, and now his brother's funeral.

The fact that he was the last of the Cosentino

line meant nothing to him. He viewed his family as cursed, which in of itself was problematic, so perhaps it was a good thing there were no more of them. He was the last, and he would remain the last, and there would be no more to grieve. No more funerals to attend. No more good people to be missed. No more guilt for being the sole survivor.

Once today was over, he'd shut the Cosentino ancestral home, sell off Marius's Argentinean estates and move to one of his smaller estates, far from Rome. Far from everyone. He was done with death, done with grief, done with caring for anyone.

Clare had cried so much the past few days she didn't think she could shed another tear, but somehow during the service, listening to the lovely eulogy for her beloved Marius, the tears started again. Tears because Marius was truly one of the best people she'd ever known—strong, kind, honest, loving. She never knew how he'd grown up to be just so loving when he'd been raised by his stern older brother, who she found nothing short of cold and disapproving, but Marius always defended Rocco, saying Rocco might not appear affectionate, but he was fiercely proud and protective of him, and would die for him if need be.

Those words, *die for him*, came to her now, and Clare cried fresh tears because it would have been better if Rocco had died and not Marius. Marius was so full of light and love whereas Rocco barely interacted with the world, living like a hermit in his monstrously big house, a house he'd inherited as a sixteen-year-old when his parents died just weeks apart from an infectious disease they'd picked up on their travels. Clare hated visiting the big dark house, but Marius would drag her there every six months for either Christmas or New Year's, and then again late July for big brother Rocco's birthday.

Rocco was never friendly on those occasions, barely speaking two words to her. When Marius proposed, her first thought was yes, yes, because she loved him desperately, but later, when she'd gone to bed that night, her new ring so wonderful and strange on her finger, it crossed her mind that now Rocco would be her family, too.

And that thought hadn't been pleasant.

In fact, that thought had kept her awake far too late.

Now she stood next to the man who'd never be her brother waiting for the service to conclude. She would be leaving as soon as they returned to the house. She had a car already arranged to pick her up and take her back to the airport. No point remaining in Rome longer than necessary. It's not as if she was wanted or needed here. Rocco didn't need comforting, at least not from her. Marius didn't have a will. The estate in Spain was all in his name. There was nothing else to be done but for her to return home and figure out how to continue without her heart, as that had been buried with Marius.

* * *

From where Rocco stood in the drawing room he could see outside to the manicured circular drive where a big black Mercedes waited for Clare.

He admired the young woman's foresight, appreciating her desire to not prolong today's events. Any mourning Rocco would do, he'd do in private. He suspected Clare felt the same.

"I see your car has arrived," he said, hands clasped behind his back.

She still wore that heavy black lace veil, but he could see the haunting lavender blue of her eyes as she looked at him. "Yes." She hadn't sat down, either. The two of them were standing still in the formal room. "I hate to leave you like this—"

"But you don't," he said, cutting her short, raw pain in his deep, gravelly voice. "We're not close. We have no desire to grieve together."

She lifted her head, and again he could see that lavender of her eyes beneath the lace. "Will you grieve for him?"

"He is all I had left." The moment the words left his mouth, Rocco felt foolish. Exposed. It was easier if others believed he didn't care or feel. Easier to let strangers believe he was as hard as he appeared. He gestured toward the tall ornate doors. "I have no wish to keep you. You mustn't miss your flight."

Her head inclined, once, and then she folded the lace veil back, exposing her golden hair and her pale face with the deep violet shadows beneath her unusual lavender eyes. "I probably won't see you again," she said, "but maybe it will help for you to know just how much Marius loved you. He said you were the best brother, father and mother a boy could have." Then she dropped the veil and giving him another faint nod, walked out of the house to the car.

That should have been the last time Rocco saw her. In any other situation it would have been, because he had no desire to be reminded of Marius, or the others he'd lost, but when the envelope finally reached him, catching up to him in Argentina where he was supervising a harvest on his late brother's estate in Mendoza, Rocco had set it aside, and then it had been covered by other papers and mail, and when he went to open it, the envelope had gone missing. He'd searched everywhere and then feared it had been thrown out. Instead it had simply been misplaced, gathered with an expense report and filed for end of the year taxes.

When he'd finally discovered the envelope amongst his tax paperwork, eleven months had passed. Opening the envelope Rocco discovered he wasn't the last of his family.

Beautiful American Clare Redmond had delivered a healthy baby boy two years ago.

# CHAPTER ONE

THE DISTINCTIVE ROAR of helicopter blades caught Clare's attention, and her hands paused over the keyboard of her laptop as she listened to the jarring hum and vibration.

The shuddering noise grew closer.

Clare listened for another long moment before pushing away from her desk to walk to the window of her villa's office and look up. The helicopter hovered now directly overhead. It wasn't high, either, but low, far too low to just be passing over. They were either looking for someone or something as the helicopter dropped lower, no longer above the sixteenth-century Renaissance villa, but appearing to prepare to land. Then it did descend, right onto the great lawn behind the villa.

Helicopters had landed at the seaside villa before with VIP guests, presidents and prime ministers, celebrities wanting a quick arrival and departure, but she always knew in advance. Her team would be alerted, security would be alerted and there would be staffing to manage the arrival and to keep other guests back for safety. But there had been nothing shared and the arrival of this helicopter made her uneasy. Why she felt uneasy, she didn't know, but her instincts were usually correct, honed by grief and work. Clare left her office and quickly descended the wide marble staircase to step out the front door.

Gio Orsini, her head of security, appeared next to her. "You know about this?" he asked, his polished bald head tipping, his gaze riveted on the helicopter filling the expansive lawn, huge blades still spinning.

She shook her head, aware that whatever it was, whoever it was, she'd meet the problem head-on. If there was anything she'd learned from her tumultuous life it was that fear couldn't be given power. Adrenaline was fine. Weakness was not.

Clare followed Gio onto the villa's broad front steps. Six months ago the villa had still been an exclusive luxury hotel, one she'd owned as part of her luxury property portfolio, but she'd discovered she was happiest at Villa Conchetti, and closed the hotel so she could make it her family home. "Is it a charter helicopter, or privately owned?" she asked.

"Privately owned I believe." Gio glanced at her. "Adriano is still asleep?" he asked.

She nodded, picturing her son napping in his nursery with his nanny in attendance.

"I will secure the nursery wing," Gio added. "But I'd be more comfortable if you returned to the house until we know who is here and why."

Gio had protected her and her young son for the past two and a half years, a constant in her life from the moment she'd left the hospital as a grieving single mom. "Give me a moment," she said. "I have a feeling I know who this is."

"*Chi, allora*?" he asked. *Who, then?*

"I'm hoping I'm wrong," she said instead. Praying she was wrong.

Gio's eyes narrowed, but he said nothing else, and she didn't, either. Seconds later the pilot climbed out, but before he could open the passenger door, it opened and a tall man with black hair and a pale olive complexion stepped out, carrying a small leather duffle bag. He was so tall he had to stoop to avoid the whirring blades and even though Clare couldn't see his face, she knew immediately who it was.

Rocco.

Her stomach fell, a sharp plummet that made her feel sick. She'd expected him so long ago. She'd written to him more than eighteen months ago but when he'd never responded, she'd finally given up on hearing from him. Instead he was here, at her villa, in person.

Clare's skin prickled with unease, and her mouth dried as her pulse raced.

"What do you want me to do?" Gio asked quietly, as they both knew Rocco Cosentino was a threat.

"Nothing for now," she said. "Just have staff remain vigilant."

"Of course."

She held her position on the front step and out-wardly she looked calm, but the wild thudding of her heart made her hands tremble. Just a month ago, in late July, she'd given up thinking Rocco would reach out. It had been so long since she'd written to him about Adriano, over a year and a half ago, she'd stopped worrying, stopping imagining an unpleasant reunion, but just when she'd relaxed and her defenses had come down, he was here, quickly approaching the entrance to her home.

"I've been looking for you," Rocco said, reaching her side. His deep voice was deeper than she remembered, but every bit as grim. His hard, chiseled features were without expression and his icy silver gaze swept her from head to toe. There was no smile in his eyes, no warmth in his greeting.

Apparently nothing had changed. "For over a year and a half, really?" She tipped her head, met his eyes, such an unusual shade of gray, more like pewter than mist. "And to think I have been so close, just twenty-four kilometers from Rome."

"You waited a year to tell me about my nephew."

"And you waited over a year to reach out." Her chin lifted, and she lifted a finger in Gio's direction and he silently retreated, not far, but giving them space. "But then, you are busy."

Rocco stepped up, joining her on the top stair. "Once I knew about the child, I hired detectives as you were not easy to find. But I think you know that." The corner of his mouth lifted, but it wasn't a smile. "Perhaps next time you'll add a return address to your correspondence?"

It was on the tip of her tongue to say there wouldn't be a next time and then she thought better of it. There was no reason to provoke Marius's older brother. She and Rocco weren't close, but as this was the first time they'd seen each other since the funeral, she didn't want to create unnecessary friction. She wanted to leave the bad blood in the past. It was her hope they could be cordial in the future.

"The birth announcement took some time to find me," Rocco said. "I was in Mendoza when it finally reached me. But before I could read the contents, the envelope was caught up in paperwork. I only found it when I was gathering my files for taxes in May."

"Have you moved to Argentina?" she asked, surprised.

"No. I spent a few months there last year trying to sort out some issues at Marius's winery. There were problems with the management, and I was tired of excuses."

"I would have thought you'd have sold it by now."

"I've sold nothing of my brother's."

"Why not? The two of you have very different approaches to your finances." Her lips curved faintly. "He liked to spend money and you don't. I can't imagine the winery is earning a significant return on the investment."

"It's not, but it makes good wines, and with proper management, it could be far more profitable." Rocco's gaze met hers and held. "But I haven't come to discuss my investment strategy with you."

She broke free from his magnetic gaze, her attention dropping, skimming his scarred left cheek, thinking it both strange and shocking seeing him here. Rocco was so like Marius in coloring…a quick glance revealed the family resemblance, but Rocco was taller and considerably broader through the shoulders and chest. Their features would have been similar if it weren't for the thick scar and burn mark on Rocco's cheek, creeping into the hairline. Even without the scars, Rocco's eyes were so different from his brother's. Marius had lovely brown eyes, warm, smiling. She didn't think she'd ever seen Rocco smile, his silver irises perpetually flinty. Frosty. But then, everything about Rocco was imposing and cold, and no one she wanted near her, or in her home or around her son.

But he'd come because of her son and she couldn't very well leave Rocco on her front steps forever.

"Let's go to the terrace," she said. "It will be more private there."

She led the way through the house's airy entrance hall to the glass doors that opened onto a secluded terrace overlooking the sea. The terrace had numerous small sitting areas, as well as a table she and Adriano enjoyed when they ate an early dinner outside. Potted citrus trees dotted the long terrace, while the doorway was fragrant with climbing roses.

"I'll have refreshments brought to us," Clare said,

choosing one of the small sitting areas in the shade and sitting down in a wrought iron chair with pale pink cushions. "Would you care for juice, a spritzer or an espresso?"

"What will you have?" Rocco asked, taking the chair across from hers.

"A spritzer," she said. "It's a warm day."

"I'll have the same," he answered.

Clare glanced at Roberto, her *maggiordomo*, standing in the doorway, awaiting instructions. "Two wine spritzers," she instructed, "and perhaps something light to eat."

Roberto disappeared, but Clare knew she wasn't without her staff. Gio was just inside the doorway, standing in the shadows. Other security were on the perimeter of the property. She took no chances with her son's safety. He was her heart and her world and everything she did was for him now.

Clare carefully crossed one leg over the other, high on her knee, the hem of her dress just touching her knees, revealing her slim calves. She felt Rocco's gaze rest on her legs, and saw a flicker of something in his eyes. She wasn't sure, but she wished she was wearing trousers and a long-sleeve tunic now, but in the warm months she preferred dresses as they were cooler and more comfortable.

"It's been quite some time," she said, voice crisp. "I'd begun to think I'd never see you again."

Rocco shrugged. "If it weren't for the birth announcement you wouldn't have."

Neither said anything for a long moment. Clare was content to leave the ball in Rocco's court. After all, he was the one who'd traveled here today. Let him say what he'd come to say.

Rocco had opened his mouth to speak when Roberto appeared with a silver tray. Rocco's mouth closed and they waited as Roberto positioned the wineglasses and little plates in front of them—nuts, crostini, a small charcuterie board.

"Help yourself, please," she said as Roberto disappeared.

Instead Rocco sipped his wine spritzer and then frowned.

"Too much bubbly water and not enough wine?" she asked.

"No. What wine is this? It's not Italian, is it."

"It's a California Chardonnay, from Paso Robles, near the Central Coast." She hesitated. "I've bought a vineyard there. Have put in some olive orchards, too. It was a good opportunity so I took it."

"You always surprise me."

"Because I'm not the silly society girl you thought I was?"

He opened his mouth to protest but then closed it without saying anything as they both knew he'd disapproved of her from the start and his opinion of her had only worsened during the time she and Marius were together. "Did the birth announcement really get lost in the shuffle?"

"I was incredibly embarrassed to discover I was the one who'd 'lost' the envelope. For the longest time I thought Marius's staff was careless, thinking it was maybe thrown out in a cleaning."

"And what did you think when you finally opened it?"

"Shock. Disbelief." He hesitated, expression grim. "It still seems impossible, especially as no one seemed to know of this…development. None of Marius's circle. None of yours, either."

"I didn't send out birth announcements. In fact, I told no one other than you, and it wasn't an announcement as much as a very brief note, because yes, he is your nephew."

"I've brought him gifts."

"That's very kind of you."

"Not kind. Essential. I am determined to make amends, as well as make up for lost time. To think I've had a nephew for years and am only meeting him today." Rocco's brilliant gaze looked at her, most intently. "When can I meet him? Is he here?"

"He is here. I never leave him. But he's napping at the moment. I still insist on an afternoon nap, otherwise he becomes a little bear, cranky and unreasonable."

"That doesn't sound like Marius."

"No? Perhaps he's inherited those traits from me." She smiled thinly as it crossed her mind they were no longer united in grief. Adriano had given her a purpose for living. His birth had centered her, strengthened her. He depended on her and she wasn't going to let anything—or anyone—harm her child.

Rocco set his flute down. "Want to fill me in on the parts I've missed?"

His voice was so gentle it made the hair on her nape rise. She didn't trust his tone, didn't trust him. Rocco was not a man to be trifled with. Fortunately, she was a woman not easily intimidated. "Which part?" she asked, crossing her legs.

"The part where my dead brother fathers a child."

Her gaze met his and held. So that's what this was about. Rocco didn't believe her. Interesting. But honestly, she didn't care. She didn't need him, or his money or his acceptance. She didn't need a damn thing from him. "It seems I conceived before Marius died."

His brow lifted. "It was possible."

Clare bit her tongue hard, holding back her indignation. She couldn't let him know how much he upset her. She wouldn't give him the satisfaction. After a moment she smiled. "Is that a question, or a statement? Can't tell from your tone."

"I just find it ironic."

"Maybe we should switch to Italian as I'm concerned about your word choices in English. It's not ironic, it's tragic." Her chin lifted, and her eyes blazed. "It's tragic that I have a beautiful little boy who will never know his father. Tragic because Marius was the one anxious for children and I was in no hurry as I just wanted to enjoy being a newlywed. Marius's bride." Her throat threatened to close but she fought hard to keep her emotions in check. "But God had different plans for me and so here we are, a mother and a son."

"And an uncle," Rocco added.

She lifted an eyebrow. "It doesn't sound as if you want to be an uncle."

"I don't want to be played, that's all."

"And why would I do that, Rocco? What would I get out of it?"

He ignored her questions and asked another of his own. "You've had a DNA test? For confirmation?"

Clare held her breath and briefly closed her eyes. She would not curse Rocco Cosentino. She would not spit at him. She would not spew a stream of livid, hostile remarks at him, no matter how arrogant he should be.

She opened her eyes and looked at him directly, her gaze locking with his. "I don't need one. I was a virgin when we met. There had been no one else in my life. Marius was my first, my only, and most likely my last. I have no desire to replace him, ever."

Rocco just looked at her, intently. But she found his silence insulting, nearly as insulting as her need to discuss her private life. "Besides, it doesn't matter what you think. Adriano is my baby, my son. I don't need to prove anything to you." Clare was so angry she was trembling, but so far she'd kept her voice even. "I think you should go."

"I've come a long way to meet him."

"*So?*" She laughed, simultaneously amused and livid. "Am I supposed to feel badly for you?"

"This isn't about me."

"No?" Clare set her glass down and rose. "You could have fooled me." She looked to the doorway where Gio stood in the shadows and nodded once.

Rocco noted her nod and growled with displeasure. "You're throwing me out?"

"We have nothing to say to each other after all."

"I want to see my nephew."

"No, you don't. You came to shame me and I won't be shamed. Yes, Adriano was born out of wedlock, but that's because his father died two days before the wedding." Her lips quivered and she could feel the hot sting of tears in her eyes, but she smiled fiercely to keep the tears from falling. "Marius always defended you, saying that you couldn't help the way you were, that you'd been hit with too much too soon, but that's not my problem. It's not Adriano's problem, either. So, no, I don't want you to meet my baby. Not today, and maybe not ever."

Clare walked away from Rocco, through the open French door to the cool interior of the villa even as Gio stepped out to deal with the guest.

Roberto shut the door behind her, standing in front of it, another sentry on guard, all here to protect Adriano, a child vulnerable to those with malicious intentions. She didn't yet know Rocco's intentions but her guard was up, and her temper was high.

Clare walked swiftly down the marble entry into one of the elegant salons she'd turned into the music room with the high frescoed ceiling with the gleaming pink and gold marble floor. She paced the room, past the grand piano, oblivious to the priceless oil paintings on the wall, and the beauty and history of a home hundreds of years old. Her heart pounded and emotion surged through her—confusion, frustration and anger. Anger that Rocco had finally appeared, but so many months after she'd expected him, more than a year after thinking he'd care. But now he was here and instead of arriving with warmth or genuine feeling, he was infuriating her all over again.

He'd always infuriated her.

She had wanted so badly to have a happy family, and share Marius's love of his brother, but Clare never could be comfortable when Rocco was around. He was hard and ruthless, like the walls of the ruined medieval fortress just down the beach from her villa. Tourists lined up to visit the ruined fortress, but she had no interest in ruins, not when she was working so hard to create a safe world for her son, giving him the stability and love she'd never known, but this focus wasn't about the past, but the future. Adriano's future. Her future. A future with hope and happiness.

"*Mi scusi*," the housemaid said from the doorway.

Clare turned at the far end of the room, pausing in front of the ornate marble fireplace surround. "Yes?"

"Ava wanted you to know that your son is awake."

Clare pictured Rocco outside, aware that he was probably still on the terrace, aware that he was thinking she would return, because really, how was the conversation over? How had they settled anything?

"Have Ava bring him downstairs to me after he's had a snack. I will be on the terrace with our guest." Clare's voice firmed. "I'd like Ava to remain close, in the event that Adriano isn't comfortable."

The maid nodded and disappeared. Clare drew a deep breath and squared her shoulders preparing for battle, because that's exactly what this was with Rocco Cosentino. He wasn't her friend. He was a foe and they both knew it.

# CHAPTER TWO

ROCCO EXHALED AS Clare disappeared into the villa. He hadn't anticipated a warm welcome, and he hadn't helped things by asking about a DNA test, but he needed to ask. He needed to know, but he wasn't going to pursue that conversation further especially as there were other ways to verify Adriano's ancestry. He just needed time to get the verification. He needed time, period. Now that he was here, it was hard to imagine just walking away from her. To be honest, he'd never walked away from her. She'd been the one to leave the Cosentino villa in Rome after the funeral. She'd called for a car, and yes, he'd put her into it, but it was the right thing to do.

Seeing her again was painful, though. Just looking into her eyes stirred up intensely conflicted feelings. Their last visit had been the day of the funeral. It had been such a dark, dark day, the grief numbing. He'd been numb for months after.

But Rocco was determined to block out the memories, and just as determined to keep a tight rein on his emotions. He couldn't allow himself to feel anything. He couldn't allow himself to be drawn into the past, with all its guilt and regret. Rocco had hated himself the day of the funeral. He'd hated himself so much that he just wanted to be buried with his brother, be over it, be done with it once and for all. Too many funerals, too much death, too much remorse, too much grief. Unfortunately, in typical Rocco Cosentino fashion, he survived the day, and said his goodbyes to Clare, and moved forward with this life, managing both his estates and his brother's, in Spain, Italy and Argentina, the Argentina property left to him by his mother.

He still remembered the moment he found the file with the birth announcement tucked inside of it.

Marius had fathered a child? There was an heir? Another generation of Cosentinos?

Could he trust Clare to tell the truth?

But why would she lie? She was an heiress herself. The two families had billions between them, a shocking amount of wealth, but that wealth hadn't protected them from loss or loneliness. The birth of a child, a Cosentino, was huge, but the fact that it was Clare's child…that was incredibly problematic.

So first Rocco needed facts. The truth. And then, if Adriano was a Cosentino, Rocco needed to remain close.

Rocco glanced now at the bodyguard who had remained on the terrace with him. The man's head was shaved smooth, his gaze shielded by a pair of dark sunglasses.

Rocco knew that the moment Clare decided Rocco was to be shown off the property he would be, but so far that hadn't happened, which gave Rocco hope that he and Clare could still have a conversation, a civil conversation.

That would require Rocco keeping his temper in check. His temper wasn't usually an issue, but from the beginning, from that very first meet, Clare had brought out the worst in him.

She made him feel, and he hated that.

She made him think—not of business, not of family, not of loyalty—but of lives not lived, emotions not experienced.

The only way he'd ever known how to function around Clare was to hide who he was, containing himself so that she didn't know him. Couldn't know him.

But that hard exterior was a sham, the walls erected to keep Clare away, distant, so that he could be detached and keep his head.

She was that much of a temptation. Still.

The French doors opened and Clare appeared on the threshold.

"Still here?" she asked, perfectly framed by the pale stone walls covered with the lush bloom of late summer roses. The pink roses perfumed the air, creating a softness around Clare that was at odds with her fierceness. She hadn't been fierce when Marius was alive. She'd been anything but fierce, leaning on Marius for his love, drinking in his devotion as if a flower deprived of sunlight.

She didn't lean now. Although petite, she stood tall, her chin up, her eyes flashing at him. Her new toughness wasn't the only change, though. Her hair was darker, the light golden strands now a rich cocoa. Her face had some color, as if she'd spent hours on the sunny terrace, or perhaps down on the sand. It would be impossible to avoid the sun when living here at the sea.

"I ask your forgiveness," Rocco said formally in English before switching to Italian, and repeating it. "It was not my intention to make us enemies. We are family—"

"We've never been family," she interrupted, walking toward him. "You never wanted me as family," she added, voice dropping. "Remember?"

The bodyguard had stepped back into the shadows and Clare now stood in front of Rocco, hands on her hips, her dark head thrown back, revealing her stunning violet-colored eyes.

She was right. He did not want Marius to marry her. He did not want her as a sister-in-law, but to admit it now was adding insult to injury. He said nothing rather than make things worse.

Her full mouth curved, a faint dimple appeared in her cheek, but there was fire in her eyes. She was not happy with him, not happy to see him. He sensed that she would have preferred to never see him again.

"You've never really talked to me," she said. "But maybe it's time we were honest. We should be truthful. We both know you never liked me." Clare held his gaze, daring him to contradict her. "Can you at least admit that?"

"How will this help anything?"

"I can't trust you if I don't know you. I can't know you if you don't have a real conversation with me. I think we both owe Marius that much. A conversation, and maybe a chance to come to an understanding."

She barely reached the middle of his chest. Her dark hair fell below her shoulders. Motherhood hadn't aged her. She was still exquisite, and still oblivious of her beauty. "These truths might make things worse," he answered.

"They will if we're wanting to wound. I do not wish to hurt you, and to be honest, I've no desire to be hurt by you. I just want to understand why…" her voice faded and she sighed, shadows in her violet eyes. "Why you tried to keep Marius and me apart."

"I didn't think you were a person of substance, and thus, I didn't think you were right for my brother," Rocco answered bluntly.

"But *why*?"

"It's difficult to articulate. The only way I can explain it is a gut instinct."

"A gut instinct?" she repeated, color deepening in her cheeks. "That's it? No proof? Nothing to substantiate this?"

"It was my job to look after my brother, and in my mind, you weren't the right one for him." Rocco's voice dropped, deepened. "I told him as much."

"You had no right."

"I had every right. I was his older brother, as well as the only father figure he remembered. I had to represent the entire family—"

She laughed, interrupting him. "That's so ridiculous," she said, walking away, leaving him to go stand against the balustrade. For a long moment she didn't speak and Rocco watched her, studying her, taking in the white dress with the dark purple trim, it was such a simple sundress, but it flattered her.

Clare turned to look at him. "Your brother was also an adult, a man, capable of making his own decisions."

"And yet he looked to me for reassurance," Rocco said.

"Because you exerted too much influence. He felt as if he had to constantly please you, but that shouldn't have been necessary. No younger brother should ever have to grow up fearing his older brother's censure—"

"That's not how it was between us, not at all."

"Then how was it?" she asked, leaning against the railing, head tipped, expression somewhat mocking.

He slowly crossed the distance between them until he was just a foot away, blocking the sun, and able to clearly see her light eyes with the lavender irises, so stunning, so unusual. Like her. He'd never met anyone like her, which was both good and bad. "Marius was my family, my world—he was very loved."

"He was also *my* world, *my* family and his death broke my heart. I will never love anyone the way I loved him, which is why I'm so careful with Adriano. He is so young, so innocent. He is to be protected, not pulled between us."

"I would never do that."

"No?" she challenged.

"No," he replied firmly. "I swear to you as a Cosentino, and on my family honor, to do what is best for Marius's son always."

She considered this and then nodded. "Good, because he will be coming down soon, and you shall have the chance to meet him." Clare gestured to the grouping of chairs where they'd been sitting earlier. "Shall we sit, and try this again?"

He followed her to the sitting area and waited for her to sit down before he sat. He waited a moment to give her a chance to take charge of the conversation but she just looked at him, waiting.

That was fine with him. He had countless questions. "I thought you were blonde," he said. "Or was that just color?"

She almost smiled. "I'm a natural blonde. When I was young I had silver blond hair, but it darkened to the gold shade in my twenties. I dyed it black after Marius's funeral. I couldn't stand looking into the mirror and seeing myself. I didn't want to be me anymore, especially as seeing my hair, reminded me of

Marius. He'd loved my hair, the pale gold color, and so every time I saw myself, I felt angry. Cheated. I covered it up. Looking back, it was my way of mourning."

"Did it help?"

"It did. I felt different. Strange to myself which helped me cope with all the grief."

"Are you still grieving?" he asked.

"I will always grieve his loss, but the fire that used to consume me is gone. The rage and pain have become acceptance…reluctant acceptance."

"I understand."

"Do you?" And then in the next moment she shook her head. "Forgive me. Of course you do. I can see it in your face, in your eyes. You're still wearing your grief, but you've lost so many people that I'm not surprised."

"And you have your son which gives you purpose."

She hesitated and then nodded. "Yes, it does. And hopefully when you meet Adriano, you will feel some of the hope I feel."

Hope. Such a strange concept, Rocco though, suddenly unable to remain seated. He rose and walked the width of the terrace, briefly glancing out past the garden to the rocky cliff and the dark blue sea beyond. "Tell me about my nephew," he said, walking back toward Clare. "Is he much like my brother?"

"He's a toddler, almost of preschool age, but in other ways, very much a baby still. It's hard to say who he's like, but he has your brother's coloring, and his smile." Her expression softened. The tension in her job easing. "Just as Marius's smile lit up the room, Adriano's does that, too. His nanny adores him. Those that know him love him. I know I'm biased as I'm his mother, but I do think he's special. I look forward to hearing what you think."

"But he's happy?" Rocco persisted.

"Very. He laughs a lot. He smiles a great deal. He brings tremendous joy to my life, and those around him." The light in her eyes dimmed, shadows returning. "I don't think I would have survived the last few years without him."

Rocco forced himself to sit, trying to contain his energy. Everything within him felt stirred—restless—and he didn't like it. He took a sip of his drink. It was no longer cold and he set it down, knowing he wouldn't try it again. "And his intelligence? Is he bright? Marius was always very smart, very curious."

"He is speaking three languages, or more accurately, he can understand three languages. I speak several languages, but only speak to him right now in English and Italian. His nanny speaks to him mostly in Spanish, which I thought important, seeing as his father loved the family home in Argentina. I thought Adriano should know the language should he ever visit."

"Thank you," Rocco said simply. "In case there's any doubt, let me reassure you, that I have no wish to take him from you. He is your son. That is not a point of contention. I am merely here to meet the son of my beloved brother."

As if on cue, a young woman appeared in the doorway and spoke to Clare, addressing her in Spanish. Clare answered the young woman in Spanish. It sounded as if the child had finished his snack and was ready to join them. Clare instructed the nanny to bring Adriano out, along with a few of his toys, and maybe the green ball he liked so much.

Ava stepped back into the house and Clare focused her attention on Rocco. "He's coming now."

It was just a minute later when a childish laugh came from within the house and then a boy burst through the door, at a run, heading straight for Clare.

He was small but sturdy, and he flung himself at Clare. "Mama," he cried, climbing onto her lap.

Her arms wrapped around him and she pressed a half dozen kisses to his cheeks, forehead and then finally the tip of his nose. "Hello, my baby, my beautiful boy. Did you have a good nap?" she said in English.

"*Sì*," Adriano said firmly, answering her English with Italian.

Rocco checked his smile, remembering how Marius used to do the same thing as a young child. He understood everything, but chose to answer in whichever language he felt like answering in.

Clare turned the toddler around on her lap, so Adriano was facing out. "We have a guest," she said, tone cheerful. "Adriano, this is your papa's brother.

This is your uncle, Zio Rocco. He has come to meet you. Isn't that exciting?"

Rocco watched Adriano's expression shift, his friendly smile growing slightly more guarded, his pale brow creasing. He had long thick lashes, a firm chin, a firm press to his lips and a dark but focused gaze.

"Adriano, it is true. I am your papa's brother. I was the big brother. I loved your papa very much."

Silence stretched. Adriano processed this, expression still guarded, no emotion evident.

Rocco noticed that Clare allowed the boy to respond when and how he wanted. She didn't hurry him, or tell him how to respond. Rocco approved.

After several long moments Adriano wiggled off Clare's lap and stood on his own two feet. His expression revealed curiosity and after another moment of scrutinizing the guest, the child crossed to Rocco with the same athletic grace he'd shown when running onto the terrace. Now he stood quite still before his uncle, scrutinizing him from head to toe. "*Zio* not *tio*?" Adriano asked.

Rocco glanced at Clare and she smiled at him, clearly proud of Adriano's perceptiveness.

Rocco was impressed, as well. "Zio," Rocco looked back at the child. "*Italiano*," he confirmed.

Adriano extended his hand. "*Mi chiamo Adriano.*" *My name is Adriano.*

Rocco felt a stab of pain thinking how much his brother would have loved this child. But with Marius gone, Rocco would do everything he could to protect the boy. He took the child's small chubby hand in his, and gave it a formal shake. "It's nice to meet you, Adriano."

Adriano gave a firm shake back, but he wasn't smiling. He looked serious, his brows pulling in concentration. Marius, for his part, was rarely serious, always quick to smile and laugh. Marius loved a joke, and although bright, found it difficult to focus on academics, excelling instead in sports. And friends. He'd had countless friends. He was a true friend, and loyal, and of course, handsome, charming and generous to a fault.

Rocco's lips twisted.

Clare spoke, suggesting Adriano show his uncle how good he was playing *calcio*, or soccer. Adriano glanced at Rocco, checking his interest. Rocco nodded at him. "*Mi piace molto il calcio*," he assured him.

Adriano seemed to approve as he finally gave Rocco a smile and with a dash he was running to pick up his ball. He threw it down the terrace, and then chased after the ball, intercepting it before it could bounce downstairs. He kicked the ball right, and then left, as if showing off his footwork. As if he himself was in a game.

Rocco couldn't help smiling, touched, and amused, because there, in the fancy footwork, in the intense concentration was Marius. "*Lui e bello*," Rocco said quietly. *He's beautiful.*

Clare nodded, sudden tears in her eyes. "He is," she agreed.

They applauded Adriano as he raced up and then down the terrace, and then finally Adriano came to his mother's side, and leaned against her legs. His face was flushed and he had a sheen of perspiration on his brow. "*Com'e stato?*" he asked his mother.

"Wonderful. You won the game, didn't you?" she answered in English.

Adriano laughed. "There was no game, Mama. It was just the warm-up."

"Aren't you tired now?" she asked, giving him a little hug.

"No." Adriano flexed his arm, showing a nonexistent bicep. "I am very strong."

"You are. But maybe perhaps you'd like a little gelato, just because you've worked so hard?"

Adriano jumped and clapped. "*Sì!*"

"Then go find Ava and tell her I said you could have one scoop of gelato. Just one, though, as we don't want to spoil your appetite for dinner. Understand?"

"*Sì*, Mama." He pressed a kiss to her cheek and then with a wave at Rocco he ran into the house, the door closing silently behind him.

Rocco hadn't even realized he'd been holding his breath until the door had closed, and then he exhaled, pain splintering in his heart. Adriano was very much like Marius in some ways, handsome and athletic, but he'd also inherited Clare's keen intellect.

* * *

With Adriano back in the house, Clare should have felt better, safer, but instead her nerves were wound tight, her shoulders tense, her insides knotted.

She was waiting for whatever would come next.

What *would* come next?

Now that Rocco had seen his nephew, would he be satisfied? Would he summon his helicopter back and leave, curiosity answered? Somehow she doubted it. Somehow she knew this was just the beginning. But of what? That was the question. This wasn't a chance meeting. Rocco had been searching for them and clearly he'd been intrigued by Marius's son…so what would Rocco want now?

Rocco left his chair and passed behind her and she found herself stiffening, as aware of him as if he'd reached out and touched her. Her skin prickled everywhere, the hair on her nape rose and a shiver raced through her. Her stomach, already in knots, lurched and she drew a slow breath, trying to ignore the wave of unease rushing through her. There was no reason she should be anxious. He had no power over her. He couldn't hurt her. He wasn't a man who hurt people—words from Marius's lips more than once. Rocco might look scarred and fierce, but he wasn't dangerous. Not to her, or to Adriano.

And yet, she wanted Rocco gone. Soon. Now.

But she said nothing, letting him prowl about, once again inspecting the terrace, the view, the ocean brilliant beneath the September sun.

"Thank you," Rocco finally said, breaking the silence. He'd walked halfway down the terrace before returning.

"For?" she asked, trying to gather her calm.

"Loving him so well. He's obviously very happy and healthy. I'm not surprised, but I am impressed. Marius would be pleased."

"I do everything for Marius."

"In that case, may I remain for a few days? I'd like to get to know my nephew better. Obviously, I have no desire to impose. The last thing I wish to do is make you uncomfortable."

Clare didn't know how to answer because Rocco did make her uncomfortable, but not for the reasons she would have expected.

Ever since she'd returned from the music room Rocco had been unfailingly polite. He'd been gentle with Adriano. There was nothing that should make her uneasy and yet she was unsettled. Her skin felt too sensitive, and her pulse wasn't quite steady. Clare didn't know why she couldn't find her center. Rocco had knocked her off balance.

And yet, how could she refuse his request?

This was Adriano's only blood relation on his father's side. Rocco could be—perhaps should be—an important figure in her son's life. "I have no objection," she said at length. "Do you intend to leave and return, or…?"

"I'll have my bag dropped off later."

"Another helicopter landing?" she said, lips curving faintly.

Creases fanned from the corners of his eyes, amusement flashing briefly in the silver depths. "I think my bag could travel by car, if that's all right with you."

It wasn't a smile, she thought, but it came close. For some reason this pleased her and her smile deepened, a hint of warmth offsetting some of the ice and fear filling her chest. "A car is perfectly acceptable," she replied, rising. "In the meantime, the staff will prepare your room. It should only take a few minutes. Would you like to wait here, or perhaps in one of the indoor salons?"

"Anywhere I won't be in the way."

"You're not in the way. I'm going to return to my office as I have a number of emails to answer before the workday ends. My staff—my company's management team—are waiting for me to respond to some questions from this morning's meeting. You don't mind me escaping for a bit, do you?"

"Of course not. I'm good to wait here. Don't worry about me."

"Gio will keep you company," she said, glancing at her head of security, suppressing a smile. "He's not very talkative, but he'll keep you safe."

"Am I in danger?" he asked, a teasing glint in his eyes.

For a moment Clare couldn't think, her mind going blank, caught off guard by this very different Rocco, a Rocco who smiled at her, a Rocco with laugh lines, a Rocco who made her feel as if she was part of the conversation instead of excluded. Her chest felt strange, tight and tender at the same time. She wasn't sure how to manage this Rocco. It was easier to dislike him, easier keeping him at arm's length.

"You're not in danger," she said, deciding truth was the best policy now. "The security is for Adriano."

Rocco's smile faded. "Has there been an issue with safety?"

In the past she wouldn't have shared anything, but she needed an ally, and Rocco could be a powerful one. She swallowed and chose her words carefully. "My father isn't well, and when he goes, his estate will pass to Adriano. Children are vulnerable, let alone children worth billions."

Rocco's expression didn't change, but his voice dropped, deepening. "You live very quietly. You don't publicize your wealth. I found it almost impossible to find you."

Her head tipped. Her smile was strained. "And yet you did. It just took you time." She turned at the door. "So you see, I must be on guard. Not trying to be dramatic, just realistic."

In her upstairs office suite which sprawled over two rooms, each giving her a different view, one of the garden, and one of the sea, Clare sat down at her desk but couldn't bring herself to even touch her computer keyboard.

She wasn't exaggerating when she'd expressed her commitment to keeping Adriano safe—and out of the limelight. Clare's childhood had been so very different. She'd been raised in the upper echelon of American society, which meant her family spent considerable time abroad, socializing with the upper echelon of European society. When you were the only child of one of the wealthiest men in America, you had access to everyone and every event.

But Clare had never cared about money. Wealth didn't make one happy. Just look at her father—he'd been married countless times and each divorce left him more bitter than the last. He always said that the smartest thing he did was to have an ironclad prenup—his wives would get whatever jewelry and property he bought them during the marriage—but that was it. He also made sure there would be no more children as he'd hated the horrendous custody battle that had occurred when Clare was young. He'd ended up having to share custody with Clare's mother, and the deep resentment on both her parents' parts would have continued throughout Clare's life if her mother hadn't died when Clare was twelve, succumbing to a heart defect that none of them had even known about.

It was only after Clare's mother was gone that her father claimed Clare's late mother was a virtual saint, and that there were no woman who could compare to her. Thus his procession of new, and ever younger, brides. Slimmer. Sleeker. More ambitious than the last.

Clare was delighted to be sent to Europe for high school and then university. Far better to live away from her father's parade of wives, women who were determined to get pregnant and remove Clare's status as Daddy's beloved little girl.

Clare enjoyed Europe, and gradually it became home. She used some of her pocket money to buy a small Paris flat, and then later she invested in a little island off the coast of Italy. It had once been inhabited but vines and drought had killed off many of the old olive trees and orchards, but Clare liked the idea of having a place of her own, and had hired a couple, and then several workers, to make the crumbling stone house habitable. She periodically sent money, and paid bills, but she didn't visit as she'd also purchased other properties that had more commercial value.

It was the weekend of her twenty-second birthday and she was on a yacht anchored off Cádiz celebrating with friends when introduced to Marius. She hadn't thought love at first sight was possible—after all, that was her father's favorite line—but she'd taken one look at him and felt as if she'd known him forever, or, perhaps, she wanted to know him forever.

They had two and a half years together, and were planning a lifetime together, when he died just days before their wedding.

The only comfort she could take in the following weeks, and then months, was that she was pregnant and at least she'd have his child. Clare hadn't wanted to know the gender of the baby, and the nurse practitioner she saw for monthly checkups kept insisting it was a girl, so it had been a shock when she went into labor and twelve hours later delivered a boy.

The baby had dark hair and deep blue eyes and a hint of a dimple in its fat cheek, the dimple almost identical to the one Marius had, that Clare cried as she held her son, missing her Marius.

The nurse had gently removed the baby from Clare's arms, saying it wasn't good for the baby to hear such grief so soon after his birth, and Clare had continued crying without him. The first six weeks were filled with tears, but gradually she recovered from her bleak depression even as her body healed. She named the infant Adriano Marius Jonathan Cosentino, after her son's father and both grandfathers, and had him baptized at six months. It was some months after the baptism that she wrote to Rocco, letting him know she'd given birth to a son and he was doing well. She'd been tempted to add, that they were both doing well, but stopped herself knowing Rocco wouldn't care.

*Had she been wrong, though?*

Clare shifted in her desk chair, sitting forward as she pictured Rocco arriving in the helicopter, as well as their first tense conversation following his arrival. He'd been searching for them, Clare and Adriano, and once he'd met Adriano, Rocco had clearly been entranced. But it was easy to adore Adriano; he was the best of all of them.

But that didn't mean she was going to drop her guard. If anything, Rocco's arrival, and request to remain for a day or two, had made her even more conflicted. She had to remain vigilant. Rocco was brilliant and still not to be trusted.

Her watch buzzed. She glanced down at the text from Gio. Her guest wanted to know what time dinner would be served.

Clare arched an eyebrow. She hadn't thought that far in advance. To be honest, she hadn't wanted to think about dinner, or having to entertain. She usually had an early dinner with Adriano and then returned to her office after he was in bed. She couldn't imagine Rocco eating dinner at five thirty, though.

She texted Gio back.

Where is Rocco now?

Gio responded.

In the blue suite.

The blue suite was on the third floor in a different wing from the family's wing, which allowed security to keep visitors from the nursery and Clare's rooms. Clare rarely had visitors, but when a university girlfriend stayed three months ago, Clare had her in the guest wing, as well.

She texted Gio.

I will go to him.

# CHAPTER THREE

ROBERTO, CLARE'S BUTLER, had shown Rocco to his suite of rooms on the third floor, but Gio lingered just outside the door, as if uncomfortable leaving Rocco unattended.

Rocco was more amused than offended and recognized that he'd handled things with Clare badly when he'd first arrived, but hopefully they were past that now. He went to the doorway and faced the bodyguard. "I have not come to cause trouble," he said to Gio. "But I was tactless. I should have reassured her first that I have only come to pledge my loyalty and protection."

The bodyguard's expression was impassive, his gaze briefly landing on Rocco and then away.

"Well, it was a good talk. I'll leave you to do your job." Rocco nodded at Gio and then closed the door, shutting Gio out.

Rocco inspected his rooms, a very luxurious suite with a living room, elegant spacious bedroom and an opulent bath, all with views of the sea. The decor of blue and white, reflecting the ocean view, the furniture antiques mixed with a few modern pieces for ultimate comfort.

He opened the bedroom doors onto the balcony and stepped outside, hands resting on the wrought iron railing, eyes narrowed against the sun. He knew that until a year ago this had been a much in demand hotel, one of those exclusive word-of-mouth resorts that charged upward of one thousand a night for a small room. This suite would have been ten times that. He was curious why Clare had turned the former hotel into a family home when it'd been a hotel for several decades now. He'd have to ask her at dinner, which reminded him, when was dinner?

He crossed through his suite and opened the door to the hall, and yes, there was his good man Gio still standing sentry. "Do you know what time I'm expected for dinner?"

"I will find out," the bodyguard answered.

"Thank you." Rocco didn't bother closing the door this time and was still wandering around the living room of the suite, studying the artwork, when he heard footsteps behind him.

"Will these rooms work for you?" Clare asked.

He turned, surprised she'd come. "I'm sorry to have disturbed you. I know you had work to do."

She shrugged. "I wasn't getting anything done. Too much on my mind." She looked up at him, her stunning eyes searching his. "This is…unsettling… having you here."

Rocco realized he liked her hair dark, the rich brunette shade made her eyes look like violets. She was even more beautiful now than before, if that was possible. "How can I make it more comfortable for you?"

She went to the pair of French doors that matched the pair in the bedroom, and opened them, letting the late afternoon breeze sweep into the room, providing warmth and the perfume of the roses below. "It's not your problem," she said after a taut silence, glancing at him over her shoulder. "It's my problem, and I'll figure it out. I'm surprisingly good at handling problems."

"And I'm a problem?" he asked softly.

She visibly stiffened. "It wasn't my intention to imply such a thing. It's that…you know…we had a complicated relationship, and even though we want the best for Adriano, we're still virtually strangers. We knew of each other, but we didn't know each other, if that makes sense."

"It does."

He joined her on the small balcony and glanced over the railing to the terrace below. His suite of rooms in this wing faced the ocean, but below were gardens, extensive gardens from the look of it. Immediately below was a tidy ornamental garden with fountains and gravel paths, marked with boxwoods in fanciful shapes. There were other gardens beyond, paths curving around the villa walls, leading to secret gardens and a cluster of gnarled olive trees in the distance. "The gardens are so impressive," he said, "I thought I'd go for a walk, but wasn't sure what time you serve dinner here."

"There really isn't a set dinner hour. With Adriano, I tend to be informal. He eats very early and in summer we've been eating outside, alfresco, or if he's tired, in his nursery. It's a gorgeous suite of rooms—possibly my favorite in the house."

"So we'll eat with him tonight?" Rocco asked.

She hesitated. "Probably not tonight. But you'll see him in the morning at breakfast, if you're an early riser, as he is."

"Why not tonight?"

"He's in bed usually by seven. He eats at five thirty, has a bath and stories. It's five now. If you'd like to eat soon I could make arrangements—"

"That is indeed early," he interrupted with a grimace. "Breakfast would be better."

He could tell she was fighting a smile. "So what time would you like to eat? Eight, nine, later?"

"What is best for you?"

"I'd prefer eight, as I'll probably return to my office after dinner."

"Do you work every night?"

Her eyes narrowed and she looked at him, as if trying to understand if there was an ulterior reason for the question. "Once Adriano is in bed, I will read, or work. I like to keep my mind busy, and I find work very satisfying. But then, I imagine you feel the same way. The Cosentino family has an extensive portfolio of investments."

"And I am the only Cosentino left. Well, until now."

"That must be a relief," she said.

She had no idea. Adriano changed everything, in more ways than one. "Dinner at eight," he said, content to leave it at that.

"I will alert the kitchen," Clare answered. "Oh, and dinner will be informal. I suggest you wear something comfortable, that is, if your bag has arrived."

"It should be here within the hour," he said.

"Perfect."

He walked her to the door, and as she joined Gio in the hallway, she paused and glanced back at Rocco, her gaze meeting his. For a long moment she just looked at him, truly looked at him, before turning and walking away.

What had that long look meant?

What had she been trying to see?

Rocco slowly closed the door, but he could still see her lovely face with those lovely lips and haunting violet eyes.

Her eyes did haunt him, as did the memory of the past. She was right when she'd said they had a complicated past. Their history wasn't pleasant, and he was the one who'd made it impossible, he was the one who'd made it difficult and she didn't even know why. He knew, but he could never tell her. He wouldn't. But that didn't mean he wasn't aware of the truth, tormented by guilt.

But with her gone, and the heavy door closed, he felt trapped, and angry. He didn't even know why he was angry only that he suddenly wanted to hit something, break something, even though he never physically lashed out. He always held emotions in. He always bottled them up, reducing those emotions until they could be ignored, forgotten.

But the emotions were bubbling up, just as the past wasn't sleeping, either. Everything seemed to have broken free, history mocking him for being an ass. Selfish. Destructive.

Rocco paced the length of the room again, as caged as a big cat in a small zoo enclosure. He couldn't do this, be here in Clare's home, pretending. Pretending he wasn't responsible for the rift between them. Pretending she was the problem, or had been the problem. Clare hadn't been anything but Clare... polite, curious, reserved and hopelessly beautiful.

He stopped pacing and drew a slow breath, trying to get a handle on the anger. He needed fresh air and perspective. He could get both, but he had to walk, move, clear his head.

This luxurious suite with its priceless antiques and dazzling view of the sea was nothing more than a gilded box.

Returning to the door, Rocco opened it, relieved to discover the bodyguard gone. Quickly he retraced his earlier steps along the long corridor to the formal marble staircase, down the stairs to the ground floor where he exited onto the terrace, and then from the terrace into the gardens. The winding gravel path appealed, and Rocco walked quickly, as if the devil was chasing, and maybe the devil was, because that beast, that monster wasn't behind him, it was in him. He was the monster and there was nothing he could do about it now.

His shoes crunched the pea gravel as he skirted the rose garden for the small orchard, and once he'd entered the orchard, he slowed, appreciating the shade.

Earlier Clare had asked about his animosity, asking him for the truth, wanting him to confirm what they both knew—that he didn't like her. She'd wanted an explanation and he'd done his best to deflect the question, not at all prepared to tell her the truth. Because he could never tell her the truth.

There was no reason for him to dislike her so much. His dislike had been immature, illogical, which only made his interactions with her more complicated.

Until Clare entered the picture, Rocco had prided himself on his self-control. His self-control had gotten him through so many difficult times, helping him manage pain and disappointment, but he wasn't in control with regard to Clare, and he hadn't been kind to her, or supportive of Marius and Clare's engagement.

It had taken him a long time to understand his animosity to Clare. But it was not something he could explain to Clare. He could barely admit the truth to himself, but he'd been hard on her because she'd elicited such a strong response within him.

He'd been drawn to her immediately, and in a way he hadn't been drawn to any other woman. Ever.

She had made him feel. She had made him want. She made him crave.

It was maddening, infuriating. How could he be so physically attracted to her, this American woman who wasn't even his?

How could his body betray him, tightening every time she was near, stirring his senses, arousing his hunger. Testing his control.

And she, beautiful violet-eyed Clare, was his brother's. His brother's girlfriend, and then his brother's fiancée, and soon to be his brother's wife. And throughout it all, Rocco battled himself, horrified that he wanted his brother's woman.

What kind of brother was he to desire someone that didn't belong to him? Someone that meant so much to Marius, the brother he adored?

How could he justify fantasizing about taking Clare's mouth, her body, filling her, owning her, making her shiver and shudder in his arms.

And yet he did.

His dreams were filled with her, his thoughts so primal and carnal he felt out of control. The fact that she elicited such strong feelings in him frustrated him, and he snapped hard on those feelings, embarrassed by the attraction. The only way he could cope when around her was to detach himself, becoming distant, even cold, but it was necessary. By freezing his emotions he could block her out, pretend she wasn't there, pretend that she didn't exist.

Marius had asked him several times why Rocco was so cold to Clare, especially as Clare had done nothing to warrant such frosty behavior, and Rocco had always simply replied that there was something about her he didn't trust, that there was something he couldn't respect, when the truth was, he couldn't trust *himself*, not when close to her.

Rocco had been married in his twenties. After his wife died, he took a mistress in Rome, but those relationships didn't prepare him for lust, for hot, raw, desire. All-consuming desire. A need that kept him awake at night, his humming thoughts burning as he imagined all the things he'd do to Clare, with Clare, if only he could.

Indecent things with his shaft and hands, his lips and tongue and teeth.

During those long nights he'd palm himself, bringing himself to frustrated climax, but the orgasms didn't ease the need. Or the pictures in his head. Clare made him feel animalistic. Untamed. Like a man who'd been starved because in his heart of hearts he thought she should be his.

In his heart of hearts he didn't believe his brother deserved her.

Every time he saw Marius and Clare together, he

felt a surge of frustration, frustration that grew into anger, anger that bighearted, good-natured, easygoing Marius had won Clare's heart.

Did his brother even understand how lucky he was?

Did his brother know that there weren't many women like Clare? In fact, there was only her, the one, and she loved Marius.

Rocco couldn't let his brother know his feelings. Worse, they were feelings that confounded Rocco, feelings that tied him in knots, and so he did his best to avoid Clare, with or without Marius.

In all fairness, when Rocco handed Clare into the limousine after Marius's funeral, it had been a relief. He'd never see her again. He wouldn't feel this awful temptation, or the impossible desire, again. He'd hated feeling like such a bad brother to Marius, hated the conflicted desire—so tragic and Shakespearean, as well as plain ridiculous—so saying goodbye to Clare had been a relief. He'd have his life back. Not life as he wanted it, because God only knew that Rocco would give everything to have his brother still with him, but at least he didn't have to struggle with guilt and remorse, and the needling voice in his head that constantly whispered that he was a terrible man. Because a good man, a man of integrity and honor, wouldn't have coveted his brother's soon-to-be wife, but Rocco had.

Clare dressed for dinner with care, showering and then once dry, slipping on a long feminine kaftan in a green malachite pattern, a deep purple sash tied at the waist. As she blow-dried her hair, the soft silk fabric brushed her bare legs and slid across her shoulders. She couldn't have worn these intense colors as a blonde, but they worked with her dark hair, and the soft purple tie at her waist made her happy. It was playful and youthful and with Rocco Cosentino here, she could use the confidence booster because she found him so very intimidating.

She didn't even know what it was about him that unsettled her, but when near him her pulse tended to race and she felt vulnerable and sensitive, which was why the long kaftan appealed for dinner—it covered her, from her shoulders to her ankles. Even the sleeves extended past her elbows, fluttering on her forearm.

Clare put on a little mascara and lip gloss, and after adding a pair of gold dangly earrings with bits of amethyst, and slipping her feet into wedge sandals, she was ready to go downstairs and entertain her guest. This was her house, she reminded herself firmly. She was the host and she wasn't going to be dictated to by Rocco. She wasn't going to be used by him, either.

She understood the way of the world and how powerful men had run society and civilization for thousands of years. She'd been raised by such a man which gave her a unique perspective, as well as a position of strength. Clare had money and power of her own. She didn't need to fear Rocco, or fear anything he had to say. His opinion was simply his opinion. She was every bit as wealthy as he, every bit as educated, every bit as confident. She didn't need his approval or his permission. In fact, she didn't need him at all.

But her cool resolve faltered as she paused outside the dining room, surprised by the dimmed chandelier, and the flickering candles on the table and in the pairs of delicate Venetian sconces.

Rocco was already there, admiring one of the seventeenth-century Baroque gilt wood floor lamps flanking the doorway. "Did all of this come with the house?" he asked, turning to greet her, dressed in a black suit, white shirt and black silk tie. "Or are these acquisitions you've made?"

It was hard to focus on his question when her heart was beating fast. She'd told him that dinner was informal, and yet Rocco looked dashing—elegant—in a stunning, sophisticated twill suit made from an incredibly fine wool. One of her newest ventures was the purchase of an Italian fashion house specializing in menswear, high-end menswear, and she was curious to know more about Rocco's suit but didn't feel it appropriate to ask.

She forced her gaze from his chiseled jaw to his strong aquiline nose, to his silver gaze beneath black eyebrows. "A combination," she said, trying not to feel like a gauche schoolgirl. She wasn't a girl, but a woman, and she wasn't a virgin, but a mother. Just because Marius had been sunshine and laughter, didn't mean she had to be cowed by Rocco's brooding intensity. "When I first purchased the villa, it was fully furnished, but as it was a hotel, I refurbished tired rooms and began to collect pieces that would fit the different rooms and decor."

"I think that's what made finding you so difficult. I was looking for a private residence, not a hotel, and I'd been under the impression this was still a hotel."

"It was until a year ago Christmas. We always closed for January and February, reopening in March, but when it came to reopen, I realized I'd rather live here full-time, and so we never reopened, and little by little I converted the hotel into what it had originally been—a private home. A family home."

"But it's so big for just two people."

Clare laughed. "I employ a small army, and most live on the property, so as you can imagine, the space comes in handy."

The chef appeared in the doorway, letting Clare know the first course was ready, if she was ready to sit down.

Clare gestured for Rocco to join her at the table. Again she noted the candles and the dimmed overhead lighting. "I'm surprised by the candles," she told him as he held her chair for her. "This isn't something Adriano and I do."

"I asked for them," Rocco answered, sitting to her right, instead of at the far end of the table. "I thought after a long day it'd be more restful."

But as the first course was served, Clare struggled to eat with Rocco so close and her pulse continuing to drum, making her feel strangely breathless. Ideally Rocco should have been seated across the table from her, instead of on her right. He was left-handed and she was right and there were moments their hands brushed and each light touch made her even more light-headed.

It had been a long day, though, and she was unaccustomed to entertaining, never mind Marius's brother who'd always been so brusque with her. She knew he didn't think she was good enough for Marius, and she'd decided that hostility would get them nowhere, but it was hard to forget the tension, hard to not resent him for making those last few months leading up to the wedding so stressful.

She and Marius could have had a wedding anywhere. They could have had a huge wedding, something lavish, even ostentatious, but that wasn't Marius's style. Despite his background, he preferred to be casual, and he'd wanted their wedding to be relaxed, fun, something his closest friends would enjoy. Since most played polo, or were sponsors of the sport, they scheduled the wedding for late August to coincide with the end of the polo season in Spain, and just before everyone shifted to Argentina for the fall. The wedding would be held at Marius's sprawling villa in Sotogrande, ten minutes from the breathtaking beaches of Cádiz, and thirty minutes from the Gibraltar airport.

The Spanish villa's gardens were expansive, as well as tropical and lush, and they'd planned to have tents erected to cover the broad lawns, while the reception would feature colorful flowers and the best music for dancing, as well as truly great food. The wedding reflected Marius's personality. He was color and passion personified.

It was there at the Santa María Polo Club in Sotogrande that Marius died, a freak accident just days before the wedding, an accident that no one could have seen coming. Everyone knew that polo could be a dangerous sport. Risks were an inherent part of sports, but for Marius to be thrown? Unthinkable.

The funeral was a blur. She traveled to her main property then, a small private island off the coast of Italy, and it was there she realized she was pregnant. She'd known in September she'd missed a period but with grief it hadn't surprised her. Her shock had almost incapacitated her. She'd stopped eating, drinking, sleeping. How could something have happened like this…to Marius of all people? He was the ultimate horseman. The horse whisperer, his friends teased him. No one knew or loved horses like Marius.

It wasn't until late October that Clare realized she'd missed a second period, and her body felt different. Her emotions felt different. She'd ordered a pregnancy test kit to be delivered to her secluded home. When the results flashed positive, she traveled to the nearest medical clinic, consulted a doctor, had a blood test done, along with an ultrasound, confirming the pregnancy, and how far along she was. She'd probably conceived the day Marius died, or the day before. They'd made love all week, but they'd been a little reckless near the end, knowing the wedding was just days away.

The baby arrived as scheduled on May the nineteenth. She'd named him after Marius's Argentine grandfather, a famous polo player just like Marius. She'd added middle names to include her father, and Marius, of course. It was a long name for an infant but Clare knew he'd grow into it, and he was.

One of the staff approached the table, quickly removing one course to return with the second. Although Clare usually loved seafood, tonight the plated fish made her stomach heave a little. She was finding it so hard to relax. Maybe sharing memories of Marius would help. Maybe it would comfort them both. "Do you remember Marius as a baby?" she asked Rocco, who didn't seem to have a problem with the Acqua Pazza.

"Of course. I was ten when he was born. It was exciting. Everybody was happy, and from the beginning Marius was easy, a very cheerful baby."

Clare smiled wistfully. Adriano had been more challenging as a baby, but Marius would have been patient with him, and wonderful. "I always assumed due to the age difference between you and your brother, Marius was an oops baby, but maybe that isn't true, maybe your parents—"

"Our mothers were different. The age gap was due to the fact that our father took his time remarrying after my mother died. But I'm glad he remarried. He married two good women. He was lucky in love."

"I had no idea Marius was your half brother?"

Rocco's eyes narrowed. "There is no half anything. He was my brother, period. My family, my world."

Clare flushed, embarrassed. "I didn't mean to imply that the relationship was less then—"

"And yet you said *half*."

"I was surprised, that is all. He never mentioned it."

"Why should he? It wasn't important, certainly nothing to discuss with an outsider."

"I was his fiancée, not a stranger."

"Family is family. There are no lines drawn, no division based on genetics. My mother died when I was about Adriano's age. I have no memory of her. The only mother I knew was Marius's, and she was wonderful. I was her son." Rocco fell silent a moment. "Children need parents. I needed a mother. It weighs on me that Adriano has no father."

"But he does have me," Clare said firmly. "He is my first priority, my only real priority. The rest is just—" She snapped her fingers. "Stuff."

"But you yourself implied you must juggle motherhood and work—"

"I wasn't complaining. I like being busy."

"But if you didn't work, you could be with your son more—"

"I am with him for breakfast, lunch and dinner, plus bath time, bedtime, and playtime after his afternoon nap. On weekends there is no nanny. It's just us." She lifted her chin, fighting anger. Who was he to judge? And if he wasn't judging, but thinking he was being helpful, he was wrong. "I'm a better mother for working five hours during the day, and it's good for him to have others to love him. No one can ever have too much love."

"But does your staff love him, or are they just paid to act loving?"

Clare bit down, jaw clamped, as she counted to five and then to ten. "Your input isn't wanted or needed, not if it's going to be so critical."

"That isn't my intent. I'm playing devil's advocate."

"Well then, please don't. It's the last thing I need. As a single parent I'm aware of the challenges, but work gives me pleasure, and it's not something I need to give up—not for you, not for anyone."

"Even though you don't need the money?"

"You work and you don't need the money," she countered, thinking that would finally silence him.

It didn't. He shrugged. "I have no family. I have nothing in my life but the family estates and portfolio. It's all I have."

"You could remarry and have a family."

He grew still, his expression almost haunted.

"I couldn't," he said after a long tense moment. "It wouldn't be right."

Clare's heart suddenly ached for him. The fact that Rocco still grieved for his wife moved her profoundly. He understood love, and loss, and honored his commitments. She wasn't sure she liked him, but at least she was beginning to get to know him. "But you have thought about it?" she asked gently, searching his shadowed eyes.

He shifted uncomfortably. "And dismissed the idea."

"Why?"

He looked away, his gaze skimming the room with the flickering sconces and the soft candlelight reflecting off the table. "It's complicated."

Still she said nothing and he glanced at her, lips twisting. "You should let it go. Suffice it to say, I don't take marriage vows lightly. Marriage is for life."

Staff returned to take their plates, removing the second course. "Dessert?" she asked Rocco. "Cheese and fruit, or something a little more decadent? I think chef has made *marizotto* for you, but there's no pressure."

"I'm actually fine without anything. Maybe just a coffee."

She looked to the server. "Just the one coffee, but we'll have it in on the little terrace." Clare pushed back from her chair and lifted her wine. "Shall we go outside? It's lovely this time of night outside."

The little terrace was her favorite place to be at night. Strands of white lights were strung across the pretty little patio garden, illuminating a fountain built against the stucco wall on one side and a wall of purple bougainvillea on the other. The patio's floor was covered in creamy travertine tiles and the furniture was comfortable—sumptuous ivory lounge chairs each with its own lavender blanket.

Clare settled onto one of the lounge chairs and covered her legs with the soft pastel blanket. "Too feminine for you?" she asked, curious as to what he'd think of her secret patio garden with the tinkling fountain and the crashing waves in the distance.

"Not at all. It's beautiful, and very peaceful. I can see why you like to come here at night." He sat down carefully on the other chair, but he didn't stretch out.

Clare studied his profile, his broad shoulders, lean muscular torso and long powerful legs. Marius had been lithe and athletic, but Rocco was powerful, with the look of a prizefighter. Strong, physical, tough. For a little bit neither said anything, but Clare was acutely aware of Rocco not far from her side, aware of the size of him, and his physicality so different from Marius.

"You're not who I thought you were," he said gruffly.

She arched a brow. "How so?"

"I assumed you were a trust fund baby. Indulged. Entitled."

"I am a trust fund baby. I've never had a real job—"

"You have a real job."

"Yes, but in high school and college I didn't have to flip hamburgers or wait tables or be a barista like other young women my age. I have always had financial security, which allowed me to be make different choices, enabling me to be successful sooner, younger."

One of the kitchen staff appeared with an espresso and a glass of sparkling water and after moving a small table closer to Rocco's chair, positioned the water and espresso at Rocco's elbow.

Rocco drank some of his water and then sipped the espresso. *"Va bene." It's good.*

"You sounds surprised."

"I'm picky about my espresso."

"I know. Marius told me."

Rocco laughed, a low husky sound that made her pulse jump, and her insides did a strange tumble. In the soft nighttime lighting, Rocco's hard features looked sculptural, all carved planes and hollows. He fascinated her tonight. He wasn't who she'd thought he was, either, and even though she wasn't relaxed, she wasn't ready to go to her room and be alone.

"And Marius once told me you were not close with your father," Rocco said.

"It's true. My father was never abusive, just… disinterested. Perhaps if I'd been a son he might have been more invested, but I even question that. My father loves himself." She looked at Rocco, eyebrows lifting. "And money, of course."

"So he didn't advise you on investing?"

"No. Never. That would be a waste of his time. In my father's eyes, women were decorative objects, pretty to look at and nice to hold, but not to be taken seriously. I wasn't to bother him, so I didn't." She smiled mischievously. "So I didn't, and I used my allowance during my university years to buy my first property, and from that early foray into real estate I discovered I liked investing, and creating a portfolio of my own. I was not your typical university student. I didn't enjoy parties, I didn't like beer, I don't drink hard liquor and, thanks to my cautious nature, I still rarely drink more than one glass of wine. I had to do something with my free time."

"I would have thought studying took up a lot of time."

"When you're reading Kierkegaard's recollection and repetition of dichotomy and the infinite qualitative distinction looking at photos of pretty properties is pure pleasure."

"Did your father mind that you were using your allowance in a different way than anticipated?"

She shrugged. "He didn't know, and I'm sure he didn't care. My father didn't want a family, but someone had to inherit, because heaven forbid the government take it all when he died, and he is not altruistic, so he isn't going to donate it to charities who could use the money. So, as the heir, I'm to stay alive, fulfilling my responsibility to him." Her lips curved but her voice cracked. "I will be donating most of his money to charity. After he's gone. I don't want it, or need it. He could have helped so many people but…" her voice faded and she didn't try to finish the sentence.

Rocco was sitting forward, forearms resting on his thighs. "And there is just you? No other siblings?"

"No siblings. Not a chance. He had a vasectomy after I was born and made it clear to his various wives that they were not to get pregnant. He didn't like the look of a pregnant woman, and he wasn't interested in having a broodmare in his bed." She reached for her wine, suddenly needing the wine to ease the lump in her throat. "You can see why Marius was so very dear to me. He was the first person that truly loved me, and not because I could do something for them, or open doors for them, but just because I was…me."

"I think there are many who will love you, for you."

She shook her head. "Not interested, not giving anyone a chance." She cleared her throat. "So, do you mind me asking how you found out about my different companies? What do you know?"

"In looking for you, I discovered your LLC, in which you are the sole owner. The corporation includes six hotels and resorts, all luxury properties catering to the wealthiest, most discriminating clients. More recently you've bought into a company that provides private jets, allowing your discriminating clients to book a private flight to their luxurious private property. And there are other companies, too, from high-tech security to farms and orchards, allowing you to diversify your investments, offset losses, better protecting your wealth."

She'd sipped the wine as he rattled off the facts. "You are quite the sleuth."

"You are the CEO. You're not just a figurehead. You actively manage your companies."

"Who knew that a girl with a degree in classical studies would have a head for business?"

He didn't smile. He just looked at her, silver gaze penetrating. "Is it hard juggling the businesses with raising a child on your own?"

"But I'm not on my own." She gestured about her, indicating the house and all within it. "I employ a virtual army to help me. Cooks, maids, gardeners, nannies, security—" She smiled. "Which you know all about because no one can do it 'all' on their own. Even if Marius lived, I would have needed help."

"Would you have worked if he'd lived?"

"I worked while he was alive." Her brow creased, perplexed. "But you knew that."

"I don't know that I did."

"What did you think I did all day?"

He shook his head. "I don't know, and it doesn't matter. My brother died a little over three years ago. It feels like a lifetime ago."

"I'm not surprised. You were such a good brother to him—"

"But I wasn't," Rocco interrupted, voice flinty.

"That's not what he said. He had so much love and respect for you."

"Don't, please." Rocco's firm mouth compressed, his expression grim. "Marius deserves the respect, not me." He looked at her then, his silver gaze meeting hers. "I live with guilt that I wasn't a better brother. I had hoped that by now the guilt would have eased, but it hasn't. It's grown stronger, heavier."

"Because you're alive, and he's not." She reached across to where he sat, and put her hand on his, but that was a mistake. The moment her palm and fingers touched the back of Rocco's hand she shuddered, shocked by an invisible current of energy that passed from his skin into hers. She quickly removed her hand, but her fingertips tingled, her palm hot, the nerve endings feeling burned. She curled her hand into a fist, pressing the sensitive skin to soothe it.

The heat wasn't her imagination, either. She could tell from Rocco's expression he'd felt the electric charge. His silver irises glowed and his heat emanated from him in waves.

Her gaze dropped from his magnetic eyes to his firm lips which had escaped the burn.

She knew he'd been burned when Marius was just a boy. Rocco, in his early twenties, had been at the wheel and there had been an accident—not their fault. If it hadn't been for Rocco's quick reflexes Marius would have been killed. Instead Rocco turned the steering wheel hard, spinning the car enough that he, on the driver's side, took the brunt of the impact. Rocco was crushed in the accident, pinned beneath the steering wheel and driver's door, and before they could free him, the engine exploded, the car quickly engulfed in fire. Marius escaped with just a few cuts and bruises, but Rocco suffered life-threatening injuries.

Marius had told Clare that Rocco never once lamented the choice he made, instead saying quietly, firmly that burns were nothing. Scars didn't matter. How could they, when Marius meant everything?

Marius said that was just who Rocco was—the ultimate protector, the perfect big brother.

Looking at Rocco now, perched on the lounge chair, a wave of dark hair falling forward on his brow, half his face chiseled with strong lines, the other half thickened with scars, she could only imagine how awful these past three years had been for Rocco.

"You've always been Marius's champion," she said, feeling remorseful. "I regret you didn't find out about Adriano sooner. I regret that I hadn't included contact details. That was wrong of me. I'm sorry. And I'm sorry for my part in the past, because I know I came between you and your brother, and that was wrong—"

"*Cara*, you did nothing wrong, and it's not your fault that Marius and I had words regarding your engagement. All I can say is that I was too controlling and it wasn't fair, not to either of you."

Inexplicable tears rushed to her eyes and Clare

blinked hard. "It seems neither of us knew each other, but Adriano has brought us together, and Marius, if he's watching, he must be happy. It's what he always wanted…us to be a family."

Rocco made a rough sound in the back of his throat.

Alarmed, Clare's gaze lifted, her eyes meeting his. "Was that presumptuous of me? If so, I'm sorry—"

"Stop apologizing. It wasn't presumptuous. You are exactly right. Marius hated the conflict between us. He'd be pleased that we're coming together—" he broke off, swallowed, expression impossible to read. "For Adriano's sake."

"But not just Adriano's," she said, tears filling her eyes. "Yours, too. You've been alone, and I am sure you've been in a very dark place. I'm hopeful we can move forward now…truly brother and sister."

# CHAPTER FOUR

ROCCO FOUND IT impossible to sleep.

Brother and sister? Is that what she saw…what she imagined?

His gut churned. He felt nauseated. He did not view Clare as a sister. He did not think of her as anything but…his. The source of his torment, the constant nagging guilt, the unattainable dream. He wanted her. He could picture the future with Clare. Making a life together, having a family with her. Not just Adriano but children of their own.

Rocco threw the light feather duvet back and left his bed, going into the adjoining marble bath to splash cold water on his face. He looked up at himself in the mirror, expression grim, determined.

He would have her. He would win her. There was no way he could lose her, after losing everyone else.

Rocco dried his face with a plush white hand towel and then turned out the bathroom light and returned to bed. But in bed, sleep still evaded him.

After Marius died Rocco was in a very dark place.

For the first six months he'd been numb, in absolute shock and denial, and then he felt so much emptiness and grief that he questioned the point in living. But when he despaired, he pictured Clare, and it was her face, her full soft mouth, her wide lavender-blue eyes that gave him strength. And hope. Not that he deserved it.

But now he'd found her again and he wanted to protect her the same way he'd always protected his brother. Was it so terrible wanting her?

He'd never touched her when Marius was alive. He'd never said anything inappropriate to her. He'd just struggled with the desire, so intense and consuming, but he'd kept it all in, kept the love and need to himself.

Could he continue to contain the desire, suppressing his love and need for her? Not if he stayed here. But how in God's name was he going to leave?

Rocco finally fell asleep sometime in the middle of the night and was still deep asleep when a knocking—pounding?—sounded on the door in the living room. Groggy, he rolled out of bed, couldn't find his shirt, and just tugged the waistband of his sweatpants higher on his hip bones before going to the door.

He opened it expecting Gio or Roberto or another member of the staff. Instead, it was Clare and Adriano, and Adriano was smiling cautiously up at him.

"We've come to ask you to join us for breakfast," Clare said crisply, when Adriano buried his face against her skirt, suddenly overcome by shyness. "We've been waiting on our breakfast, hoping to see you, but we're getting hungry." Her hand went to the top of her son's head and she lightly ruffled his hair. "If you wouldn't mind company this morning."

He saw her gaze drop to his bare chest, and lower, to where the sweatpants he wore in bed hung precariously low on his torso. He carried a lot of muscle, lean muscle, but scars covered much of his chest, up half of his neck, and most of an arm. He was so used to the thickened skin that he forgot others might feel uncomfortable, but Clare didn't look uncomfortable, curious more than anything.

"I should have put on a shirt," he said gruffly as Adriano turned to look at him again, the child's smile not quite steady.

"Who hurt you?" Adriano asked in English.

Clare shushed Adriano, but Rocco didn't mind. "I was in a car accident," Rocco answered. "There was a fire."

The little boy was staring at the burns, examining them. "Did you cry?"

"A little bit," Rocco admitted.

Adriano nodded, clearly thinking. "Did the doctor give you a shot?"

"Several."

"I don't like shots," Adriano said.

"I don't, either."

Clare cleared her throat. "I take it we woke you up."

"Yes. I had trouble sleeping last night, but give

me five minutes and I'll meet you for breakfast. Dining room?"

Adriano turned to his mom. "*Possiamo mangiare fuori?*" he asked. *Can we eat outside?*

"*Sì.*" She smiled at him and then looked up at Rocco. "I think we'll have breakfast on the terrace. It's where you first met Adriano yesterday."

"I remember."

"We'll see you soon then." She steered Adriano away and they walked down the hall hand in hand and Rocco watched them for a moment, before closing the door.

Something was different about Clare this morning but he didn't know what it was, at least not yet.


It was a beautiful morning, the sun warm and bright, the sky a vivid blue with not a cloud in sight. September was Clare's favorite month in Italy. The temperatures were warm but not humid or hot, and the garden was in full bloom, all the flowers a riot of scent and color.

Clare sat at the table on the terrace with Adriano on one side of her and Rocco on the other. The breakfast dishes had been cleared, but they were lingering in the glorious sunshine unwilling to break up the party yet. Adriano, who tended to be shy with strangers, had decided Rocco was someone he liked, and chattered away to his uncle in a mix of Spanish and Italian with a little English thrown in. Rocco, to his credit, understood everything and usually answered in Italian, but sometimes would switch languages, too.

"Mama," Adriano said, turning to look at her. "Do you have to work today?"

She hesitated. "I should."

"Could we go to the *castello* today?" he asked, eyebrows lifting, expression hopeful. "*Zio* would like it."

She checked her smile but it was difficult to resist Adriano when he looked at her with that sweet face. He had a serious side, but he also could be terribly charming, as he was now. "But maybe your uncle doesn't like castles," she said.

Adriano looked at Rocco. "Do you like castles? We have a big one near here."

"Have you seen it before?" Rocco asked him.

"One time. But maybe we can go today and then it's this many," Adriano said, holding up two fingers.

Rocco glanced at Clare, amusement in his eyes. "Should we make it two times?"

She thought of the work waiting for her, and yesterday's unanswered emails. The hotel manager in Galway that had threatened to quit. The decisions needing to be made after the staff management meeting yesterday morning. But then there was this beautiful son of hers who deserved all the happiness in the world. It was difficult sometimes juggling everything, but her son always came first. Every single time. "Yes," she said, then laughed as Adriano jumped out of his chair and cheered. "But I need a half hour. Can we do that? Adriano, you need to go to Ava and brush your teeth and put on walking shoes. And Rocco—" she broke off, flushed.

"Yes?"

Clare shook her head, embarrassed, realizing she didn't know what she was going to say to him, only that she'd wanted to include him. "Nothing. I'll see you in thirty minutes."

The massive castle was just two kilometers from the villa. It dated back to the sixteenth century, but before that, there was another fortification on the same spot, a fortress from the Middle Ages. The castle's foundation rose high from the rocks, and the castle walls and buildings stood tall, pale gold stone outlined against the brilliant blue sky. Unlike some *castellos* this was intact, the heavy walls, smooth round towers and narrow windows beautifully preserved. As it was early and midweek there were very few tourists. Gio had accompanied them to the castle and he kept pace with Adriano as the child burst into a run as they entered through the front entrance.

Clare watched Adriano stop and examine a tall wood door, the door studded with iron. Clare and Rocco caught up to Adriano and then together they went through the door to the stairs that curved inside the tower. The stone steps were narrow and high and Rocco offered his hand to Adriano who happily took it. Together they climbed to the fourth floor where the stairwell opened onto a walkway leading to the next tower.

Rocco was explaining features of the castle to Adriano, and Adriano nodded, eyes wide. She'd brought him here a year ago but he'd grown so much since then, and his understanding of things was greater and he asked Rocco questions which Rocco answered.

Gio was now at her side and she thought it was interesting how Gio had been in their lives since Adriano was born, but Gio rarely spoke and only interacted with Adriano as security, not family, and Adriano even at two and a half, could tell the difference.

They climbed stairs and peeked at things, exploring for an hour and a half before Clare could see that Adriano was growing tired and it was getting close to his lunch. She suggested they return to the villa and all readily agreed, but Adriano looked happy as he'd learned new things today, and the castle had been dramatic and full of possibilities, especially for a young child with energy and a vivid imagination.

Back at the villa, Clare, Adriano and Rocco had a picnic lunch down on the villa's private beach, and as Adriano had brought his green ball down with him, Rocco and Adriano kicked the ball up and down the sand until Adriano drooped with exhaustion. Ava, who'd been waiting at the house, was summoned and she came down to take a yawning Adriano up to the nursery for his afternoon nap while Clare and Rocco remained on the blankets on the sand.

"He'll sleep well," Clare said, her lips curving as she watched Ava lead Adriano up the stairs. She couldn't look away, her heart so full. Adriano was changing daily. It was exciting to watch him grow up, thrilling being his mom.

"You're a good mother," Rocco said quietly.

She turned to look at Rocco and there was something in his expression that made her breath catch, air bottling in her chest. She felt a shaft of sharp emotion, emotion she didn't understand, but it made her realize how alone she'd been these past few years. Yes, there was staff, but they were all on payroll. She had no family, no friends; it was her and Adriano against the world.

And now Rocco, which just made her chest ache all the more.

"I do love that little boy," she said after a moment, voice hoarse.

"He knows it," Rocco said, "and love is the most important thing at this age. Love creates stability and confidence."

Clare's eyes burned and she blinked. "You should have been a father."

"I got to be father and brother to Marius."

He glanced away, giving her his profile, the one without the burns and it was so hard and masculine—the cheekbone, the jaw, the flat black eyebrow over his silver eyes—and she felt a little shiver of appreciation race through her. In a different life she might have been drawn to him. In this life she...

Clare swallowed, stopping herself, unwilling to continue the thought. There was no point. It was too unsettling. Just thinking about a different life made her feel scared. Unsettled. She couldn't be attracted to him, or anyone. It wasn't her future. She and Adriano were tight. They were a team.

"It was a good morning," Rocco said, shifting the conversation to a neutral topic.

She nodded. "A wonderful morning," she agreed. "It felt so good to be out enjoying the day." Clare slipped her hand beneath the edge of the blanket, digging her fingers into the sand. "I sometimes forget that we're right here on the beach. We should get out more."

"Why don't you get out more?" he asked, leaning back on his hands, legs stretched in front of him. "Is it because of your workload?"

She shook her head, her gaze traveling up his legs, which were long and muscular, even in the dark denim which hugged his powerful thighs.

Blushing Clare glanced away. "I think I fall into a routine and forget how much I enjoy—and Adriano enjoys—excursions. Sometimes it seems easiest to remain at the villa. It's spacious and safe. There's a big lawn for Adriano to play on. We have this private beach. There is also a pool, but that is indoors, which is nice in winter but unused this time of year."

"Can Adriano swim yet?"

"Yes, but that's because he had lessons since he was one. It was something I insisted on as we live so close to the sea."

"You are always thinking of the dangers," Rocco said, his voice low.

She looked at him, feeling raw, and shy, as if she'd just been caught changing, revealing more of herself than she should. "Because the world is full of dangers."

"Would you feel this way if Marius was still alive?"

Hot tears pricked her eyes and she drew a deep shuddering breath. "But he's not." She blinked and a tear fell, sliding down her cheek.

Rocco leaned toward her and wiped the tear away. "So what is your plan? You and the child alone together, forever?"

She felt the swipe of his thumb all the way through her, his touch so tender that it made her long for a life not yet lived. "I will never love again," she said huskily. "Marius was my soul mate. He was my love, my best friend, all I ever wanted. I will never replace him. I will never even try."

Rocco's expression was sympathetic and kind. "Your lovely Adriano should have more. A father. Brothers and sisters—"

"I've thought of that. I've thought a great deal about him being an only child. I was an only child, and I hated it. I was lonely, but I do have options, should I want to give him a sibling. I can use a sperm donor. Many women have children without being married or in a significant relationship. There's no reason I can't."

"True. You could do that, and it would give you control. You wouldn't have to share the children with anyone, and you wouldn't have to compromise, but what if you were sick, or there was an accident… what would happen to the children? Do you have a backup plan?"

Clare didn't answer. She'd thought of that, but also dismissed it. She was young, and healthy. In her mind, she was indestructible. But perhaps that was dangerous thinking. She, who planned everything, should be planning for the worst-case scenario as well, worst case being that she also died. Her insides knotted thinking of her own mortality. Obviously, accidents happened—she only had to think about Marius—but she wasn't going to go through life afraid. "I don't play extreme sports. I'm a good driver. I'm quite healthy. I don't plan on getting sick."

"Does anyone plan on getting sick?" he retorted, but his silver gaze was warm, his expression intent, but there was no mockery in his expression, just concern.

She looked at him and then couldn't look away. His silver eyes captivated her, the deep timber of his voice mesmerizing. She didn't know this Rocco Cosentino. He'd never shown this side of himself to her. Marius had always said he was protective. Genuine. But all she'd experienced was coldness, brusqueness. Obviously here was the Rocco Marius had adored.

She was beginning to understand why Marius had loved his brother so. But why had Rocco hidden his kindness from her?

"You mean to remain here always?" Rocco asked lifting a handful of sand and squeezing it in his palm. Living apart from society in your own walled fortress?"

"It's not a fortress, it's a villa—"

"You know what I mean."

She laughed incredulously. "This isn't a prison, Rocco, it's rather like heaven with the orchards, and gardens, the ocean and extensive lawn perfect for games of football."

"But who does he play football with? His security details? Come on, a child needs friends. Companions. Tell me you will at least send him to the local school."

Her shoulder rose and fell. "I plan on hiring tutors for him. In America many children are taught at home."

"And you think that will be a happy life for him?"

Heat suddenly swept through her, making her speak sharply. "What do you know of a happy life? Marius said you had experienced so much pain—"

"I have lost too many people, and after my brother died, I wasn't sure I could take anymore, but I am still here. I am still trying to live."

"And love?" Her eyebrows lifted. "You could have more, you know. You don't have to live in isolation."

"Touché. If you don't approve of isolation, why raise Adriano apart from the world? He shouldn't be alienated from society. He should grow up surrounded by family, friends."

"But I have no family. Just my father in Florida and he's not long for the world—"

"Has he met Adriano?"

She bit down into her bottom lip, pain sweeping through her. She could only shake her head, unable to speak. Her father's indifference toward his own grandson had crushed her.

"Your father wouldn't meet him?" Rocco guessed.

"No." She held her breath a moment, pushing away the sting and the rejection. She'd vowed she'd never let her son know just how unfeeling his grandfather was. "You are the only family he has other than me."

"Then it's good I've come," Rocco said rising.

She watched him step off the blanket and walk to the edge of the water, his gaze out on the horizon where the blue sky met the darker blue-green sea.

After a moment she got to her feet and crossed the sand, joining him. He was like a magnet, she thought, pulling her to him. But maybe it was because she wanted to be near him. She liked the company. Liked *his* company. She couldn't say he made her feel safe, but it did make her feel, and it was… something she didn't understand, but it was strong, almost electric, much like the jolt she'd felt when she'd touched his hand last night.

"I will give him friends," she said after the silence had stretched too long. "When he's older."

"Why not now?"

"He's still very young, not yet three."

"Children benefit from friends at all ages."

She nodded out at the sea, and then glanced to the right and left, which was all her property. "Where would these playmates come from? The village is four kilometers away, but it wouldn't be comfortable having strangers here."

"I agree. But Adriano is very bright. If he can speak three languages now, he's ready for playmates. The bonds of friends and family are important to emotional growth and well-being."

Clare had grown up very alone, and her loneliness had been like a wound, festering, aching, and it wasn't until she'd been sent to a boarding school in Europe that she finally met girls her age, and made her first friends, and with time those friends became a makeshift family. "I don't disagree. But as a single mother it's not easy, especially as I've no interest in dating let alone remarrying."

"But you were never married," Rocco said softly.

Clare flinched, going hot then cold. "Semantics," she choked. "And you know what I meant."

"I do." Rocco walked a little way down the beach, his back to her as he stared out at the ocean, hands thrust into the front pockets of his jeans. His shoulders were wide. His posture was erect. He reminded her of a Roman general surveying his troops.

"I have tried to give him everything," she said, raising her voice to be sure he could hear. "Adriano is not deprived of anything."

"But a father," Rocco replied, turning to face her.

She inhaled sharply, eyes widening. "That's cruel," she said, "even for you."

He held her gaze, expression inscrutable. "Am I cruel?"

"You can be, and you were, putting so much pressure on Marius, trying to break us up—"

"I didn't," he gritted.

"You did. Maybe you never said to him, 'she's not good enough for you,' but you implied it in a dozen different ways. I still don't know why you objected to me, but let's not pretend now that you supported our marriage."

Rocco's faint smile faded, his silver gaze disturbingly intense. "You're right. I did not."

"Why?"

"I wanted—"

Whatever he was about to say was interrupted by Gio's shout. She couldn't hear what he was saying but she glanced at her phone which was buzzing on her wrist. Urgent, read the text. A call from the States.

"I'm needed in the house," she said looking at Rocco, meeting his silver gaze and holding it. "But this conversation isn't finished."

* * *

Rocco watched as Clare hurried across the sand, the breeze picking up tendrils of her dark hair, the full skirt of her pale blue sundress with the tiny embroidered daisies swishing around her legs as she rapidly climbed the stairs to the villa's terraced garden. He'd come so close to telling her the truth, to saying *I wanted you for myself.*

He wanted her to know how strongly he felt about her, but it'd blow up in his face. It'd be a disaster. She wouldn't be comfortable with the truth, or him. No, some things were best left unspoken.

But that didn't change how he felt, and it didn't change his desire. The years apart had only made the want and need stronger.

There would never be another for him now. It was Clare or no one. That's all there was to it.

Two hours later he was in the spacious library on the first floor reviewing financials when he received what could only be called a summons to meet Clare in her office. In Rocco's world no one summoned him so it intrigued him to be at Clare's beck and call. She was comfortable in her villa. She felt safe here. He wondered, though, what it would be like to have her feel a little less controlled, a little bit out of control, her mind and body overwhelmed by pleasure.

Her office was on the second floor in the wing opposite where his rooms were. A bodyguard was positioned at the top of the stairs and he escorted Rocco to Clare. When she opened the door, afternoon sunlight poured in through the tall windows, creating a halo of light around her. She'd changed into trousers and a black knit top, her long hair pulled back in a sleek ponytail. She looked businesslike and no-nonsense and even more beautiful.

She stepped back to let him enter the room before closing the office door behind him. "Thank you for not keeping me waiting," she said crisply, returning to her desk and sitting down. She gestured at a chair on the opposite side of her desk. "Please."

He sat, trying not to feel like a schoolboy called before the headmistress.

"I shouldn't have called you cruel," she said, not wasting time getting to the point. "You've spent your life devoted to your family, and you were an exceptional brother to Marius. He would be so happy you're here now, spending time with Adriano. He would love to see you and Adriano playing football, and just talking about things. I'm grateful, because as you say, Adriano doesn't have a father, and I don't want to deprive him of anything—"

"So don't," Rocco said quietly, interrupting her. "Give him a father."

"And where do I find such a man?"

"You could marry me."

Clare's lavender eyes grew huge. She blinked and stared at him, lips parted in shock. "But...you don't want to be married. You've made that abundantly clear."

"I don't wish to date, and I don't wish to start

over. But you're not a stranger, and you have a son that needs a father, that could benefit from a family. From me."

Rocco hadn't come here expecting to say any of this, not today, and certainly not now, but the moment seemed right and he seized the opportunity. "I understand this would not be a love marriage. This is about being practical, and proactive. We can give Adriano a family—the structure and safety—as well as the heritage and traditions that are part of his Cosentino legacy. Culture and heritage are the very heart of my family, and I am confident it is what Marius would want for his son."

Just hearing him say Marius's name made her heart ache. "We live together...but as strangers?"

"Not strangers. Family, and partners, raising Adriano together."

Her jaw worked. Fear darkened her eyes. "You want him."

"I want to be part of his life. He's the only family I have. Is it so strange to think he is important to me?"

"I worry you'll take over his life."

"Did I do that to Marius?"

She chewed on her lower lip and Rocco waited, wanting to give her time, knowing that if he came on strong and exerted too much pressure she'd feel threatened and reject his suggestion out of hand.

A minute ticked by, and then another. Finally Clare spoke. "Forgive me for being blunt, but I don't see what I get from this? I like my life with my son. I like how it is now. We're content—"

"For now. But what about later, when he is older? Have you thought about that? Children without fathers are vulnerable. Boys can be ruthless."

"Not just boys." Her gaze met his, her expression somber. "Girls can be equally ruthless. If not more so."

"Then protect him from that. Give him two parents who can love him and protect him."

"But I can't replace Marius."

"You needn't replace him," Rocco said quietly. "It would be impossible to replace him. But you could at least give his son the appearance of family."

"Exactly what are you proposing?" she asked, her voice equally low.

She had not said no. She had not shown him to the door, or demanded her security drag him out. "Marry me." Rocco's gaze met hers. "Take my name. It is already Adriano's last name. No one will think twice about his parentage. It will be assumed—"

"That you are his father?" Her voice rose, not high, but it was sharp, and brittle. "But you are not his father. And I will not have him thinking you are his father—"

"I would never presume."

"You presume now."

"I'm talking with you. We're brainstorming, discussing different possibilities for Adriano and his future. Having raised a little boy before I believe now is an ideal time to make changes, should you want to make changes. But if you don't..." He shrugged and left it at that.

She started to rise and then sat down again. Clare had gone white, and her naturally pink lips and lavender eyes were the only color in her pale face. "You've caught me off guard. I don't know what to say. This isn't something I expected, or even wanted to happen." Her eyes briefly met his before looking away, guilt suffusing her because time was passing and change was needed, but it was so hard to let Marius go. "I will always love Marius."

"I will, too, but here is the terrible, awful, painful truth. Marius is gone. Adriano will never know him. He will never know Marius's laugh or his big hugs. He will not be taught how to ride by one of the greatest polo players in the world. He will not have the memories we do. But Adriano can have different memories. You don't have to deprive him of a father figure. I can be there for him, just as I was for Marius."

She reached for her glass of water, hand trembling. She took a drink and then another before setting the glass back down. Her expression was stricken. Clare used her knuckle to wipe beneath her eyes, knocking away the moisture. "Wouldn't he be so confused? That he goes from knowing no one in his family to I'm suddenly married to his uncle? Isn't it rather appalling? It's like a Shakespearean play and the very suggestion makes my skin crawl."

Three years ago he'd thought something similar, but Marius was gone now, and Rocco desired Clare more than ever. "I have no desire to confuse Adriano. That is not my intention. We can marry and take things slowly so that everyone can adjust. There is no need to traumatize anyone—you or him."

"A marriage of convenience?" she asked, words clipped.

"Eventually I'd like Adriano to have brothers and sisters." Rocco hesitated, taking his time, wanting her to be able to process it all…as much as she could. "I loved being a big brother," he added. "It's a privilege, and a responsibility, one that would benefit Adriano, even if he feels a little jealousy at first. It is normal, you know."

Her mouth opened, closed. Rocco now knew she'd been an only child and she'd hated it. She wouldn't want Adriano to grow up alone. But Rocco wasn't going to push now. Now was the time to ease back and let her think. Her mind had to be reeling.

"I need time," she said, no longer pale, but rather flushed, her cheeks filled with hot pink color. "I have to think."

"Of course."

He hesitated and then rose. "Was there anything else you wished to discuss with me?"

She looked up at him, expression stricken, confusion evident in her eyes. "No," she whispered.

He nodded and walked out.

# CHAPTER FIVE

CLARE HEARD THE door close behind Rocco but didn't see as she'd put her head down on her arms on her desk, hiding.

She felt sick, heartsick, her body heavy and leaden. How could he suggest such a thing? How could he come here and after just one day propose to her?

How dare he?

And how could she even consider it because, God help her, she was.

Otherwise she would have shot him down on the spot. She would have laughed in his face. She would have told him to leave—and stay away. But she hadn't done any of those things.

If she married Rocco it would be for Adriano. It wouldn't be for her. It'd be to, as Rocco said so succinctly, protect Adriano and to raise him as a true Cosentino, something she couldn't do on her own. She wasn't a Cosentino. She wasn't Italian. She wasn't aristocratic.

But Rocco was nothing like Marius…and it had been easy to love Marius. Marius had been light and laughter, humor, warmth, security. She hadn't had a lot of that growing up and meeting him had been a revelation. He'd added so much to her life in so many ways. She couldn't imagine ever replacing him. She hadn't wanted to replace him, and to contemplate replacing him with his older brother? A man that didn't make her feel safe…a man that made her feel, but it wasn't a brotherly emotion, or a brotherly attraction. She shouldn't be attracted to Rocco, and yet there was this curiosity humming through her, an awareness that made her feel alive again.

But desire…she didn't trust it.

Perhaps if the marriage was just a marriage in name only it wouldn't be so overwhelming, but Rocco thought Adriano should have siblings. And Rocco was a physical man and she couldn't imagine him being okay with a platonic arrangement.

She couldn't imagine either of them surviving such an arrangement.

But to make love to him? To become Rocco's?

Clare suppressed a little shiver, sensation rushing down her spine, making everything in her feel tingly.

To be fair, she and Rocco didn't have to get intimate to make a baby. They could go the IVF route, use fertility doctors and all, specialists who'd put the sperm and egg together, saving them from becoming physical with each other. The thought calmed her.

There were options. She didn't have to panic, and

brothers and sisters for Adriano would be wonderful. Built-in friends—lifelong playmates—and a bond that would be stronger than anything else in the world. Clare did like the sound of that. She liked the idea that Adriano would have someone else in his life, someone who would be both friend and family, someone close to his age who would be in his life even when his parents were gone.

Her phone pinged, the alert reminding her she had a conference call in five minutes. Clare left her desk, refreshed her sparkling water and sat back down trying to mentally ready herself for the call, but all she could really think about was Rocco's proposal.

Forty-five minutes later, Clare left her office and exited the house to cross the long stone terrace and take the stairs down into the garden. She smelled jasmine and the heady fragrance of the late summer roses, and she inhaled and exhaled the perfume trying to clear her head, hoping to find a little bit of peace and calm.

She shouldn't have agreed to let Rocco stay. He hadn't done anything wrong, but she no longer felt easy with him here. They'd had a wonderful morning, breakfast together, and then the visit to the *castello*, followed by a picnic on the beach...but now her heart was racing and she felt panicked.

She couldn't lose her son, not to Rocco—not to anyone. If she were completely honest, that was her biggest fear. Having been so alone and lonely as a child she'd always wanted family, her own family, one that she could cherish and shower with love, attention and affection. She would raise her children differently than she'd been raised. She'd make sure they knew they were the most important thing in the world, and nothing, and no one would come between her and them.

Would Rocco truly sneak Adriano away? No. But she couldn't help worrying—what if her son ended up loving Rocco more than her? What if Adriano preferred Rocco over her?

It was childish of her, but Clare had never felt safe, and loved, until Marius entered her life, and then after a few wonderful years, he'd been taken from her and she'd felt abandoned all over again.

Miracle of miracles she was pregnant…and Adriano came into the world like the angel he was, helping heal her broken heart, helping give her purpose. And laughter. And love.

Because of Adriano, she loved and was loved.

But what if…what if something did happen to her? What would happen to Adriano? She couldn't leave him orphaned. She couldn't leave him without family. Parents.

Heart aching, Clare walked through the elegant boxwood garden and sat down on a bench facing the elegant eighteenth-century fountain with its marble Poseidon in the center, and reclining maidens in different pools.

Rocco.

Marius.

What was she to do?

If only her anxiety would ease. She needed to calm down and slow her racing pulse. There was no reason to feel frantic. Nothing bad had happened, and no one was forcing her to do anything. Rocco wasn't pressuring her, and he wouldn't hurt her. He wasn't a threat.

So why was she afraid?

Why was she so full of adrenaline and emotion?

Was it because he reminded her of Marius? Or was it because he had suggested change—life-altering change?

Or was it because Rocco was unlike anyone she'd ever met…intensely masculine, so masculine that she couldn't ignore his physical energy?

When he'd come to the door this morning he'd been shirtless, and yes there had been scars, but the scars weren't what held her attention. It was the musculature, the powerful chest, the narrow waist, the hard ripple of abs disappearing into the waistband of his pajamas, which barely clung to his lean hips.

Then on the beach, she'd been so aware of his hips and his thighs, and how the denim shaped to his quadriceps and she'd glanced up higher, to the zipper and how he'd filled his jeans there. He was a man, fit and virile, and she didn't want to think of sex, but he made her feel sexual. He made her wonder what it would be like to make love again, to be touched, and kissed, and not just by anyone but *him*.

This was why her heart raced with adrenaline

and emotion. Because the more time she spent with Rocco, the less she thought of Marius. They were two very different men, and she felt very different with Rocco than she'd felt with Marius. Marius made her feel safe, and snug. Loved and wanted. Rocco made her feel naked. Vulnerable.

Being around him rattled her. Sitting at the same table, or on the same blanket, made her hands shake, and her pulse thump and her stomach do crazy flip-flops. She wasn't afraid of Rocco, so why was she so affected by his proximity? Why did her mouth dry, and her heart race and her skin prickle as if it had become painfully sensitive?

Because...

And she knew the answer but couldn't admit it. Wouldn't admit it.

Clare jumped up off the bench and circled the fountain before passing beneath the rose arbor arch to enter the formal rose garden laid out in intricate shapes with hedges and roses and delicate purple and white ground cover.

Suddenly Clare wasn't alone in her garden. She knew by the tingling sensation at the back of her neck, fine hair rising at her nape. She glanced over her shoulder, and there Rocco was, in the garden behind her.

"Did you follow me here?" she asked.

"No. I've been out walking and am on my way back to the villa. Don't mind me," he said. "I'll just continue on."

"No, it's okay. I was thinking of you." She blushed. "Well, your suggestion anyway."

"But if you want to be alone," he said.

"I've been alone," Clare answered. "Now I'm just restless. And thinking. My brain is spinning."

"I can only imagine."

"When do you need an answer?" she asked.

His broad shoulders shifted. "Whatever makes most sense. In my mind, the sooner the better, at least for Adriano. He'll benefit from the change, in every way possible. But for you, this is all such a shock. You need time."

"But give me too much time and I'll pack us up and run away!" she joked.

He smiled faintly. "Many a truth was said in jest."

"Yes," she agreed. "I'm rather overwhelmed."

"Then let's not discuss it anymore. Let's take the proposal off the table and focus on other things, like what could we do with Adriano tomorrow? He certainly seemed to enjoy himself today."

"He did," she agreed.

Rocco was silent a moment. "When Marius was a boy, he loved the zoo, which makes me wonder if Adriano has been to the Bioparco di Roma lately?"

Clare shook her head. "He's never been to Rome's zoo."

"It's in the Villa Borghese gardens and is the best zoo in Italy."

"Adriano would love it," she said.

"Good. Why don't we do that tomorrow and keep

things light…no pressure, no decisions, nothing but creating some happy memories for Adriano."

"I think that's a wonderful idea."

Clare couldn't remember ever going to the zoo herself. She hadn't wanted to confess such a thing to Rocco, but the next day as Gio parked—he'd insisted he'd go, and drive, but promised to follow at a discreet distance—Clare felt a surge of eagerness and excitement. She felt almost as happy as Adriano who skipped between her and Rocco as Rocco handed over the tickets and the four of them entered the zoo grounds to be met by one of the zoologists overseeing Rome's zoological garden.

The zoologist turned out to be an old friend of the Cosentino family, having gone to primary school with Marius, with an older sibling that had known Rocco. Marilena was delighted to give them a private tour, including behind the scenes where some of the new zoo babies were being zealously observed and nurtured.

They learned that the zoo was over one hundred years old, designed by Carl Hagenbeck who believed animals should have open spaces and moats instead of small cages, a novel idea in 1911. Over time Rome's zoo became one of the leading zoos in Europe, surpassing even Paris's and Berlin's which still had the old system of cages. But the war put the zoo into decline and many thought it wouldn't survive, but in the nineteen-nineties the zoo was reimagined as a zoological garden, a place of education and conservation, not just entertainment.

At the primate exhibit Marilena let them into a small glassed-in area behind the public space where they could observe one of the chimps holding her new baby. They watched the new mother with the tiny infant for a long time, and Adriano stood, hands pressed to the glass, awed.

"The baby is just a week old," Marilena said, "and since the mama is a first-time mother, we wanted to give her lots of privacy."

"But can't she see us here?" Clare asked, voice low.

"It's an observation mirror," the zoologist answered, looking down at Adriano since she noticed he was listening closely. "It's a special glass that lets us see in, but none of the primates can see us."

With the tour over and Adriano wilting a little, they were invited to join Marilena for a special lunch on the lawn by the lake in the Villa Borghese grounds. Pizza was provided and Adriano happily chomped on his pizza while Marilena and Rocco visited. The sun made Clare sleepy and she closed her eyes for a moment, only to feel a tap-tap on her arm. She opened her eyes to find Adriano smiling into her face, a smear of red sauce on his cheek.

"Wake up, Mama," he said.

She yawned and glanced around, feeling guilty

she'd been a bad guest, but Rocco and Marilena were gone, and it was just Gio, Clare and Adriano.

"Signor Cosentino walked the *signorina* back to the zoo office," Gio said.

"Was I asleep long?" Clare asked, running her fingers through her hair, still sleepy and trying to wake up.

"A long time," Adriano said.

Gio checked his smile. "Just a few minutes."

Rocco returned ten minutes later with gelato for all, even Gio, and Adriano sat cross-legged on the blanket eating his gelato with great relish. Clare exchanged small smiles with Rocco, aware that Adriano's face and shirt revealed his lunch, but the little boy was so happy there was no point trying to tidy him up when he was still licking the ice cream cone.

Finally it was time to head back to the villa and as they returned to the car, Clare felt a warmth in her chest that was new, the warmth a mix of hope and a fizzy sort of happiness that was so very different than the usual oppressive weight she carried within her—grief, and worry, and exhausting responsibility.

It felt good to share life with someone. It felt good to know that there was another who cared about Adriano's well-being.

"Thank you for organizing the private tour," Clare said as they settled into the back of the Mercedes SUV. "That was really special."

"I'm sure Adriano's been to many zoos—"

"He hasn't," Clare interrupted, taking a baby wipe

from her purse and cleaning off Adriano's face and hands. "This was his first zoo trip." She glanced at Rocco and added shyly, "Mine, too."

Rocco looked stunned, but she returned her attention to Adriano's hands, making sure they were no longer sticky, before belting him into his car seat.

Gio drove them back with quiet efficiency, Adriano in the car seat in the middle of her and Rocco. Adriano had taken Rocco's hand and fell asleep holding it.

Rocco didn't pull his hand free, not even once Adriano slept, mouth open, long lashes resting on his sun-kissed cheeks.

Clare felt a pang as she glanced at the two of them. Seeing Adriano and Rocco together made her realize just how much Adriano had craved a father figure in his life. Not because she wasn't enough, but moms were different than dads, and Adriano was definitely all boy.

Back at the villa, Rocco carried the still sleeping Adriano up the stairs to the nursery where Ava waited for him. Clare took a quick shower and changed into a fresh sundress, drawing her hair back in a loose ponytail. She went downstairs to find Rocco and he was there on the terrace studying the sea. "Would you like an *aperitivo*?" she asked him.

He turned to face her. "No, thank you."

She could tell something was on his mind. His jaw was set and his gaze shuttered. Had there been an incident when he carried Adriano to the nursery?

"Did something happen?" she asked, going to stand next to him at the terrace railing. "I can tell something has upset you."

"Not upset," he answered, voice deep. "I just feel...grateful."

"Grateful?" she repeated.

He glanced down at her, his brows pulling. "I didn't think I'd ever have this feeling of family again. I didn't think I'd ever be part of a family and it's wonderful but also bittersweet."

She searched the hard planes of his face, the scars almost invisible to her now. "Why bittersweet?" she persisted, thinking she knew the answer but wanting to hear it from him.

"Because you are not mine, and Adriano isn't my child to care for. This all could be gone tomorrow."

A lump filled her throat. Her eyes felt hot and gritty. Rocco was alone, very alone, and she was lucky to have her son. "Even if we didn't marry, you'd still be in our lives. You'd still be his *zio*."

"True," he said.

Clare heard a note of pain in Rocco's voice that made her chest tighten and her heart ache. This was becoming increasingly complicated. She didn't know what to do anymore, didn't know what was right, or best. "I haven't decided," she said honestly. "I didn't even think about your suggestion today. Instead I just focused on us, at the zoo. It was lovely, all of it, from start to finish."

"It was a good day."

"A very good day. Adriano was the happiest I've ever seen him. His joy gave me joy." She reached out and lightly touched Rocco's arm. "I am considering your suggestion. I just need time. I don't want to give you a rushed answer and have it be the wrong answer. I want to consider what's best for all of us."

His dark head inclined. "Me being here will only create unnecessary pressure. I should go and give you space. Take as much time as you need to make the decision that is best for you and Adriano—"

"And you," she interrupted softly. "I want what's best for you, too."

The shadows were back in his eyes. "Then that is easy. You and Adriano are best for me. Having a family to love would be my choice, but I don't want my needs to influence you. This isn't about me. Take time. I'm in no rush."

"What if I need days?"

"Fine."

"Weeks?"

"Fine."

"And what if I don't?"

He laughed, the sound low and surprisingly warm, the husky timbre sending a shiver down her spine. "Then you don't." He leaned toward her and pressed a kiss to her forehead. "I'll leave my contact details in my room. Let me know when you want me to know…whatever it is."

He walked away from her, his long legs making short work of the terrace. Clare watched him disappear into the house, her heart in her mouth, baffled by the alternating waves of relief and regret washing over her. She was glad he was going, glad he'd agreed to allow her to figure out what she wanted, so why did she feel this way?

Lost? Abandoned?

But that didn't make sense. She wasn't being abandoned, and yet her eyes burned and her heart hurt. She blinked hard clearing away the tears. If only the world wasn't such a hard, confusing place!

Dinner that evening was challenging. Adriano was quite upset that his *zio* had left him without saying goodbye. Furthermore, why did his *zio* leave at all?

"Sweetheart, Uncle Rocco has his own home," she explained. "He has work, just like I do, and so he returned to Rome so he could get his work done, but we'll see him again, I promise you."

Adriano's chin jutted, his expression mutinous. "He should have said goodbye."

"That would have been better, yes."

"Why didn't he?"

"Well, that may have been my fault," she said carefully. "He knew I had a lot on my mind and I think he was trying to make it easy for me."

Adriano's hand gestured as only an Italian could gesture.

Clare just looked at her son, uncertain how to handle him like this. She'd never seen him so fierce and fiery and after a moment she began to eat again, hoping he was ready to move forward and let it go, but as the minutes passed, he continued to sit there, arms folded across his chest, his face that of a martyr.

Finally she set her fork down. "Adriano, why won't you finish your dinner?"

"I'm mad."

She suppressed her smile. "I know. I can tell."

He looked at her, dark eyes bright and indignant. "I finally have an uncle, Mama, and he leaves."

"He will be back you know."

"When?"

"A week? Two? I don't know, but it won't be that long—"

"Call him." Adriano pointed to her watch which he knew she sometimes took calls on.

She laughed even as tears burned the back of her eyes. "Can we finish dinner and then I'll let you call him?"

Adriano studied her for a moment than nodded. "Okay."

The moment dinner was over Adriano jumped up and pulled her to her feet, leading her upstairs to where her phone was charging on her desk. Clare had a strict policy of no phones during family time and so when they entered her office Adriano ran to her desk and unplugged it, then handed it to her.

Clare was just about to tell him she had to find his uncle's number when she saw the business card in the middle of her desk. It was Rocco's card, with a number scrawled on the front.

Her heart fell a little, a swoosh that made her breathless.

"Call, Mama," Adriano urged her.

She smiled at him and then pushed the numbers and waited. The phone rang, and rang and rang. "I'm going to have to leave a message," she said to Adriano, anticipating getting Rocco's voice mail, but then at the last moment Rocco answered.

"Hello?"

"It's Clare," she answered, putting a hand to her chest, trying to slow the wild beating of her heart. "Adriano was disappointed you didn't say goodbye to him. Would you mind talking to him?"

There was silence at the other end of the line and then Rocco cleared his throat. "Of course. Put him on."

Clare handed the phone to her son. "He wants to talk to you," she told Adriano.

Adriano put the phone to his ear, but after glancing up at her, he gave her a look that made him look thirteen instead of almost three, and then walked away, the phone still pressed to his ear. "Zio Rocco?"

"*Sì*," Clare heard Rocco say before Adriano had moved far enough away so that she couldn't hear anymore.

A few minutes later Adriano walked back to her, holding the phone out, the call ended.

"Well?" she said to him.

"Zio is going to take me to the coliseum."

She took the phone and placed it on her desk. "Where?"

"In Roma!" Adriano frowned at her. "Don't you know?"

Laughing at his indignation she wrapped her arms around him and hugged him tight. "Come on, let's go get ready for your bath."

After getting him ready for bed, tucking him in and kissing him good-night, she returned to her office and checked her phone for the text notification that had come in earlier while she'd been with Adriano in the nursery.

Don't worry about anything, cara. Try to get some sleep.

Clare read the text a second time before closing out of text messages and turning off the phone and slipping it into her pocket.

What a crazy few days. Was it really only three days ago that Rocco's helicopter landed on the lawn, turning her world upside down? How could Adriano have become so attached in such a short period of time? It didn't make sense. But then, life rarely made sense.

Leaving her office, she switched off the light and then headed up another flight of stairs to the floor she shared with Adriano. Her suite was just off the stairs while Adriano's spacious nursery was at the back. Adriano would be sleeping now, or almost asleep, and she wasn't needed, not when Ava was there.

Feeling at loose ends Clare went into her suite and closed her door, leaning against it. Easy for Rocco to say, try to get some sleep. She wasn't going to be able to sleep, not after a day like today, not when her emotions were all over the place.

She did go through the motions of getting ready for bed, though, a bath, pajamas, teeth brushed, but once between her covers, she couldn't even close her eyes.

Marry Rocco?

He'd been her enemy for years. He'd made her life so difficult. He'd made her relationship with Marius beyond challenging.

Marius hadn't understood the coldness between them. Rocco was Marius's hero. How could Clare dislike him? What could she dislike about him?

She couldn't articulate her dislike or mistrust, not to Marius, and so she and Marius had agreed it would be better to let Marius and Rocco meet without her. And Marius... Marius loved her so much he accepted this, spending time with Rocco when Clare was traveling for business. It was an arrangement that suited all of them. The brothers could enjoy each other without tension, and she could get her work done without feeling guilty that she'd deserted Marius.

Not that Marius needed constant companionship.

He was far more extroverted than she was and had a large group of friends, fellow polo players and friends from his university days, even ex-girlfriends who had stayed on good terms with him despite the romance being over. Clare didn't worry about him being with any of them. Marius was true to her. Their bond strong, deep. They were family to each other. Family was respected, protected.

Indeed, their friendship and commitment to each other was so strong that it held primary importance in their relationship, making everything easy. Effortless. Perhaps their lovemaking hadn't been adventurous, but their connection had been deeply satisfying. He'd shown her more affection in their few years together than she'd known in her entire life. His hugs, the way his arms wrapped around her, the way he held her to his chest, and kissed her temple and said something sweet, his lips curving, a smile in his voice, had been everything. Truly. His hugs were the best thing she'd ever known. Those hugs meant more than the sexual act itself. An orgasm was fine when she had one, but what she craved was Marius's warmth, and Marius's affectionate nature.

Just remembering put a lump in her throat and a sting in her eyes. She missed him so much. She missed everything about him.

In life Marius radiated calm, acceptance, encouragement. His validation had changed the way she'd thought about herself. It had changed her. Love was so powerful, so transformative that she'd become graver, stronger, more hopeful because of Marius's love.

But Marius was gone. She didn't want to ever replace him. But what about Adriano? What about what he needed?

Two days passed since Rocco had left. Clare hadn't spoken to Rocco since Adriano had wanted to call him. There had been no more texts.

She was glad as she needed the distance, as well as some calm. Clare was exhausted—mentally, emotionally, physically. At night she couldn't quiet her thoughts enough to drift off and stay asleep. Instead she'd toss and turn and then finally fall asleep but would wake abruptly, heart pounding, mouth dry. She couldn't do this.

Rocco wasn't the right one for her. Rocco wasn't her person at all. And yet she could picture his face, and his pewter eyes, glowing with heat and life.

On the third night after he'd left, she left her bed in the middle of the night, turned off the security alarm at her French doors and stepped out onto her balcony and looked up into the sky as if she could read the stars…

What would Marius want?

She searched the sky in case Marius was trying to send her a message. What would he say to her now?

Would he approve of her marrying Rocco, or would it upset him? That was the real question. Part of her thought he would sanction it, as he, like Rocco, was fiercely devoted to family. He'd be glad Rocco was there…taking care of her and his son.

It took four days before Clare had an answer for Rocco. He'd left her, giving her space, but after she'd texted him to say she wanted to discuss things with him, he replied with a message that he'd be there that evening after work.

Hearing a car approach she left her desk and went to her office window overlooking the front drive. It was a car she'd seen before, a pre–World War II Alfa Romeo, classic and rare, the exterior the palest butter yellow, and the interior a warmer caramel leather. Marius had given his brother the car for Rocco's birthday—she couldn't remember which—and Rocco had at first refused the gift, saying it was too expensive, too much, too extravagant for a man about to become a family man. But Marius insisted, and Rocco gave in and kept it, and watching Rocco now park and climb out, dressed in a dark smartly cut blazer over a white shirt, the shirt unbuttoned at the collar, Clare was glad. She was glad he had the gift from Marius, glad that they'd loved each other so much. Two brothers united against the world…at least, until she appeared. She'd nearly driven a wedge between them. Thank goodness they'd found a way around it. The last thing she wanted was to create pain for either of them.

Clare leaned closer to the glass watching Rocco

approach the villa's front door. Gio descended the steps, intercepting him. At the very same moment her watch buzzed with a security alert. She pressed the green clear, and Gio moved aside allowing Rocco to enter.

Clare left the window and walked into the marble bathroom adjacent to her office and smoothed her dark hair, combing it back behind her ears. She didn't look herself in the eyes, not wanting to see what might be there. Instead she slicked on some dark pink lipstick, and dabbed a bit of the color on her cheeks, trying to hide her paleness. She hadn't slept well in days. She hadn't been eating very much, either. Both responses were typical for her, a natural response to stress, but still, she didn't want to look like death as she met Rocco in the salon downstairs.

He was waiting for her on the terrace, his back to the doorway, facing the sea. The Cosentino brothers were both athletic, but Rocco's shoulders were broader, and his legs longer. Rocco's height coupled with the width of his shoulders made him imposing, even without looking into his cool silver eyes set in that very chiseled face.

Fortunately, he already had a glass of something amber. A neat shot to help ease into the evening. She was glad someone had already provided him with a drink, one less thing for her to worry about. Her staff was exceptional that way, and in every way. They were highly trained and very loyal, and paid well for their loyalty.

"Was there a lot of traffic leaving Rome?" she asked, stepping from the villa into the late afternoon sunshine, the golden rays stretching long across the stone terrace. She lifted a hand to shield her eyes. In a few minutes the sun would drop, but for now, the glare was almost blinding.

Rocco turned to look at her, his gaze studying her intently, the movement temporarily blocking the setting sun. "Nothing out of the ordinary. In fact, I made good time." His gaze now swept from the top of her head to her feet, and up again. "You look well."

Heat rushed to her cheeks, the surge of warmth making her light-headed. She shifted one of the chairs so she wouldn't be looking into the sun's long, piercing golden rays, and dropped into it, then crossed her legs affecting an air of calm. She didn't feel well in that moment. Her heart was racing and her stomach was somersaulting and she didn't even know how to begin the conversation they needed to have.

Roberto arrived with a glass of wine for Clare and she took it with a quiet thank-you. "Are you driving back tonight?" she asked, looking over at Rocco.

"I'd hoped to return tomorrow, after having breakfast with you and Adriano. If that met with your approval."

She nodded, fighting a bubble of panic. Could she do this? Could they?

"Good. I'm looking forward to seeing Adriano. How is he?"

"Well." She hesitated, before adding, "He's asked

about you every day. You certainly made an impression on him."

"Has he already gone to bed?"

"Just before you arrived, yes. He'd wanted to stay up to see you, but I wasn't sure what time you'd get here."

"I'm sorry. I should have called and given you a time I'd be arriving. That was thoughtless of me."

The apology was nice, but it was hard to focus when Rocco was prowling around the terrace reminding her of a big cat pacing a cage. A gorgeous big cat. She'd never noticed before that Rocco was every bit as athletic as Marius, but with a different power. Marius was one with his horses, a perfect partnership, whereas Clare couldn't imagine Rocco on a horse. He needed his feet planted, the earth grounding him.

Rocco was walking toward her, but instead of joining her, he walked behind her. She felt him behind her, too, and she shivered, sensation streaking through her, skin tingling, breasts aching, her belly tightening. The awareness was unlike anything she'd ever felt before and she peeked over her shoulder watching Rocco reach the end of the terrace. He leaned over and picked up Adriano's favorite green ball. He tossed it up, once, twice, and then lightly tossed it so that it rolled past the sitting area and gently came to rest near one of the French doors.

"What's his favorite color?" Rocco asked, moving toward her.

"Green," she said, as he passed so close behind her that the hair on her nape rose and delicious prickles ran up and down her arms. He was an arm's length away, but she could feel him as strongly as if he'd reached out and touched her, his fingertips running across the back of her neck.

Clare drew a quick, unsteady breath, nerves taut, every fiber of her being awake. Alert. Aware of him. It was so intense, dizzying really.

What was he doing to her? Did he even know the impact he had on her?

Rocco retrieved his crystal tumbler with the splash of amber liquor. Instead of sitting down in a chair, he perched on the edge of the coffee table, hands clasped between his legs, forearms sinewy. His legs were so long his knees were nearly touching hers. She glanced at his strong hands, his fingers wrapped around the glass, and then to his hips and the fit of his trousers, fine black wool snug on muscular thighs, the black leather belt around his hips, and then below the buckle, the thickness, evidence of his masculinity.

She swallowed and looked away, blushing furiously. She wasn't a virgin and she shouldn't feel shy, but she did.

She felt emotions she couldn't understand. Emotions that made her realize just how hard the past three years had been. She didn't want to be sad, not anymore.

She didn't want to be grieving or alone. She wanted more. Rocco was offering more.

Wound tightly, she jerked and her knee bumped his. His eyes met hers and held for an impossibly long moment and time slowed. His eyes weren't cold, the silver irises with bits of bronze and gold. She dragged in a breath and his gaze fell, focusing on her mouth which had gone dry.

Parched, she touched the tip of her tongue to her upper lip. Her pulse was pounding so hard now, but her body felt treacherously weak, as if her bones had melted and she was just heat. She couldn't move if she wanted. There was no way to escape him and in that moment she didn't want to, the fire beneath her skin burning hotter and brighter chasing away the coldness she'd carried with her these years.

He leaned in, his broad shoulders close, filling her vision. "Are you okay, *cara*?" he asked.

His voice was so deep and it burrowed inside her chest, filling some of the emptiness. She nodded, her gaze focused on the faint shadow of a beard on his jaw and the firmness of his mouth. His mouth intrigued her. He smelled good, too, rather intoxicating, and she forced herself to nod, even manage a faint smile. "I'm getting by."

He put a finger beneath her chin, tipping her face up to his. "Just getting by?"

She didn't know why her eyes burned and a lump filled her throat. She was strong. She didn't just fall apart, but Rocco was unraveling something inside of her and she couldn't pull herself back together fast enough. "It's been a strange week."

"It has," he agreed, thumb stroking her cheek. "Scared?"

"If I say yes, nothing will ever be the same."

"Such is life, full of change. But not all change is bad. Change can be good."

She searched his eyes. "Is this good?"

"You tell me." With another caress to her cheek and jaw, he leaned in, and covered her lips with his.

The pressure of his mouth made her pulse leap, the jolt of electricity immediate, making her mouth soften and tingle. She made a soft whimpering sound and Rocco took advantage of her parted lips to deepen the kiss even as he drew her from the chair onto his lap. She couldn't resist, the sensations intense, her body melting into his.

It was a kiss unlike any she'd ever experienced. It was consuming and hot, so hot she trembled against him, helpless, mindless, wanting more of everything, wanting all he offered and as his hands touched her, shaping her, stirring nerve endings she'd forgotten even existed, she felt almost desperate. Nothing made sense. The world didn't make sense. But as long as Rocco kept kissing her and making her feel so sensitive and alive, she wouldn't complain.

It was impossible to know how much time passed. Minutes? Hours? But by the time Rocco's head lifted and he gazed down into her eyes, his silver eyes now smoky with desire, she felt almost drunk on sensation. She'd never been kissed like that, kissed so deeply that she'd forgotten who she was, or where she was.

"So," he said, his voice deep. "What do you think?"

"I think you know how to kiss."

"And the rest of it?"

Her gaze dropped to his lap, to the thickness of his shaft pressing against the wool fabric. "I don't know about the rest of it."

He laughed lowly. "I'm talking about the future. About Adriano. About us."

He might as well have dashed some cold water in her face as she blinked and returned to her senses.

She was on his lap. Her lips were tingling and throbbing. Her body was humming, too. She slid off his lap and returned to her chair, drawing her knees up as if to create a wall between them.

She needed a barrier, something to provide defense.

"You said you've given it thought," he added calmly, looking relaxed and perfectly in control. "When you called it sounded as if you'd made a decision."

"I had." She swallowed. "I have. I've thought about everything a great deal. As you know, I was an only child and I hated it. I used to pray for a younger brother or sister, someone to keep me company, someone to play with in the nursery. I don't want Adriano to know the loneliness I knew. I don't want him to be an only child." She frowned, her brows pulling. "But I need to take this slow. This is a huge change. It's scary."

He placed his hands on her knees and left them there. "Which part is scary?"

Her shoulders rose and fell. "All of it?"

"We have tomorrow, we have the day after, we have weeks and years ahead of us. We can take our time, get to know each other. There is no rush."

"Do you mean that?" she asked, hope rushing through her, easing some of her tension. She was someone who needed order and safety, and the idea of marriage, which represented a loss of control, filled her with overwhelming anxiety.

"I do. Why would I want you to feel nervous or unhappy? How is that good for anyone?"

It was a good question, and her shoulders relaxed and she managed a small smile. "Maybe we could talk some more in the morning?"

"The morning sounds good. We'll get some sleep and then discuss whatever it is you wish to discuss."

# CHAPTER SIX

In the morning they had breakfast with Adriano on the terrace, and then while Clare handled a few business matters, Rocco played football on the lawn with Adriano. Adriano wanted to do something together, all of them like the day they visited the *castello*, but Rocco told the child that Rocco needed some time to discuss things with his mother.

Adriano reluctantly accepted this and Ava stepped in to play football with Adriano while Rocco went in search of Clare. Knowing she'd probably be in her office he went there first, and knocked on her closed door. She called for him to come in, and opening the door he stood on the threshold and watched her typing on her keyboard, fingers flying, brow furrowed in concentration.

She looked up at him after a moment and almost looked surprised to see him there. "Have you been waiting long?"

"Not that long."

"I was trying to find a diplomatic way to answer a less than diplomatic email."

"Did you?"

"I hope so. I hit Send." She wrinkled her nose as she smiled. "I don't tend to overthink those things. Just do it and be done with it. I can't stand a full inbox."

He liked looking at her, liked listening to her, too. She was beautiful. Her dark hair was loose over her shoulders, and her short-sleeve blouse, a shade of cool mint, brought out the lavender-blue of her eyes. "Could you tear yourself away from your computer for an hour or two? I thought we might go for a drive. It's a beautiful day and I have my convertible."

She glanced at one of the windows and then back at him. "I'd like that. Let me just grab a light sweater and sunglasses."

"I'll be down at the car."

"I'll meet you soon."

She was quick, too, outside in less than five minutes with the sweater, sunglasses and a purse. She'd pulled her hair back into a ponytail and changed her shoes, now wearing pretty sandals that tied around her ankles.

"Where are we going?" she asked as he held the passenger door for her.

"I thought we'd go to Ostia Antica, and we can decide what we feel like once there. We can explore the ruins, have lunch or just enjoy a coffee."

"I've never been," she said. "But it's a place I thought Adriano would like to go."

"It's quite big, and there's so much to see that I propose we drive—"

"Do you think there will be a lot of tourists?" she asked.

"There will probably be buses for tourists coming in from Rome, yes."

"Could we maybe go somewhere else? Just drive north, or south? It will feel good just to have the sun on our faces and the wind in our hair."

"We shall go north then, maybe to Ladispoli?"

"Another castle in another seaport town."

"So you know it?" he asked.

"I do, but I haven't been in a couple of years and I'd love to see if my favorite bakery is there. They made the best bread and pastries."

"We can go find out."

It was a pleasure to be driving the Alfa Romeo, especially with Clare sitting beside him. Rocco didn't try to make conversation, and Clare seemed happy to just soak up the sun and let the world pass them by. It was a scenic drive too, small villages dotting the coastline, the water a sparkling blue.

He liked having her in his car, at his side. He was ready to move forward, making a life with her. Marriage. Intimacy. Family.

He hadn't thought he'd ever marry again.

But now she was here next to him, Rocco was amazed and alarmed. Had he wished for this? Had

he craved her so much that he'd set in motion a series of terrible events? Part of him knew life didn't
work that way. The rational part of his brain knew
Marius's accident on the polo field had been just that,
a terrible accident, but Rocco had spent his life taking care of his brother, protecting him, providing for
him. But now, to be here, in this place, with this opportunity to have a family with Clare and Adriano,
created the terrible tension within him.

Now he was the one who felt as if he didn't deserve her.

Now he struggled with guilt and self-loathing.
He could marry her, become her husband, stepping
into Marius's vacant position. But was it right? Was
it fair to any of them?

If Clare knew the truth, if she understood that his
coldness and reserve had been motivated by jealousy,
she'd be appalled. As she should be. But that didn't
make him want her less. It didn't make him drop
the idea of marriage. If anything he was even more
determined to have her, claim her. And he meant to
claim her—heart, mind, body, soul. Desire hadn't
faded. If anything, it had just grown stronger. When
she was close, he felt alive, almost as if he was multi-
dimensional, everything right and fierce, everything
driven and focused.

He hadn't thought it was possible to feel this way
about another person. He hadn't wanted anyone like
this before, and even though he'd been married, he

and his wife had been childhood sweethearts, growing up together and he'd loved his wife, but it had never been this fierce, consuming desire he felt for Clare.

Clare made him feel incomplete, as if she was the other half of his soul, and this certainty gave him patience. He'd wait for her, for as long as need be.

The sense of rightness—not morally, but physically, spiritually—helped his self-control. He didn't want to frighten her. He wanted her to feel safe with him, and to trust him. Trust took time. Trust was important so that when she was finally his, she'd give all of herself to him, not just the broken pieces, but all the pieces, all the hopes, all the pain, all the dreams.

That was his plan, and the goal. And he had to succeed, otherwise guilt and Marius would haunt him forever, and that would be a terrible outcome for him...for Clare...for all of them.

Clare had no idea of the heaviness of his thoughts as Rocco was outstanding company that day. A good driver, he put her at ease, and the warm air and sunlight made her relax and tip her head back, savoring all that was good.

She didn't unplug very often. She stayed busy to keep from thinking or feeling too much, as truth be told, she worried about things, worried about the future. She tried to do everything well, but it was impossible. There were always things that slipped through the cracks. She prayed Adriano would have all his needs met, but she was human and he would grow up and need more than her one day. He'd become a boy and require an education and he'd have to find his place in the world. She just prayed he'd find the world easier than she had.

Rocco glanced at her. "You were smiling a few moments ago. What happened? What are you thinking?"

She turned her head toward him and smiled faintly. "How can you read me so well?"

"I have always been aware of you," he said simply. "Even when I didn't seem sensitive."

"You mean, even when you were beastly?" she teased.

He grimaced. "Especially then."

"But why?" she asked, facing him more fully, or as fully as she could with the seat belt holding her secure. "I'm sure you know why. Can you try to explain?"

"You won't like it. I don't like it."

"Try me."

"I was jealous. Jealous that you and Marius had found so much happiness."

"Oh, Rocco! I'm sorry," she said, putting a hand on his arm. "That was never our intention."

"No, of course not. It was my problem, not yours."

"But no one likes to feel like a third wheel, especially when you and Marius had been so close."

They reached Ladispoli far more quickly than

Clare liked. It had been wonderful being in the car, feeling free for the first time in ages, especially as a tour bus was parked at the *castello* and hordes of people wandered around with cameras.

They escaped the crowds by taking a walk along a seawall and it was there Clare brought up his proposal, which had been constantly on her mind. "*If* I agreed to marry you, Rocco, you misunderstand I am not ready for a physical relationship. You are essentially a stranger and I need time to get to know you. It might take a long time before I'm comfortable around you. Perhaps years. I don't know. You'd need to be patient with me, and patient with us becoming a family as it won't be natural or easy. Adriano will adapt relatively quickly, he's just a baby, but…" She swallowed hard. "I will need more time. The physical makes me uneasy. I know we kissed, but there's a big difference between a kiss and being naked."

*Especially with you*, she mentally added. Rocco was so intense and the sparks between them were overwhelming. She didn't want to be overwhelmed. She craved the safety she'd known with Marius.

"I am not marrying you because I can't find sexual partners elsewhere," Rocco said calmly. "I'm not marrying you to please to gratify some sexual need. I'm proposing marriage to provide permanence and stability for Adriano. I am marrying you so that he will have a father, not that he didn't have a father, but a father who will be present, a father who will love him, and be there to support him, always. You and I might not always see eye to eye, but I hope we can agree to put him first, and focus on doing what is best for him."

Clare leaned against the wall, stone rough but warmed by the sun. "I feel exactly the same way."

"Good. He doesn't need to be caught up in adult dramas. It's confusing for children and unfair to be pulled between two people who should be mature."

She glanced up at him, trying to see behind the sunglasses shielding his eyes. "You sound as if you speak from experience."

Rocco shrugged. "My parents—my father and Marius's mother—had some quarrels in the year before they succumbed to their illness. The quarrels were loud and carried. I was old enough to know that the storm would pass, but it was hard for my brother to hear the fighting and storming around."

Clare had heard plenty of yelling as a child, only it was her father who did the shouting, and her father who gave the commands. The women in his life never really stood a chance. It was one of the reasons she loved Marius so. He was easygoing and nonconfrontational. Marius hated conflict and they'd never really had a fight—neither of them wanted one, and so if things grew tense, they just moved forward. She wondered now how that would have worked if he'd lived. Was that the best way to handle problems in a marriage? "I've only had one significant other, and that was your brother. He was my first real boyfriend, and my only sexual partner." Clare stared out at the ocean as she shared this, embarrassed by the revelation but thinking it important Rocco know and understand. "I've been a late bloomer my whole life, and I hadn't wanted to be intimate with anyone until I met him. I can't even imagine intimacy with anyone else."

*Much less you*, she silently added.

The words were never spoken aloud, but they hung in the air between them.

He nodded after a long moment, his gaze sweeping over her, a slow scrutiny from head to toe. "When we marry, there will be no one else in my life, no other woman, just you. I think it's important you know that."

His scrutiny made her hot, and her skin prickly. "But maybe there should be," she said, flushing, "because if it is years until I am comfortable with you, I'd hate to think you're being denied…company."

"I'm a man, not a child. I can handle desire. I know how to manage needs. That should not be your worry—"

"It's not my worry," she interrupted tersely, pushing away from the wall. "I just don't need one more thing to feel guilty about."

Silence followed, the silence so long and heavy that Clare found herself squirming inwardly.

"What do you feel guilty about?" Rocco asked.

She lifted one shoulder. "It doesn't matter."

"But it does. It's important to understand how

you're feeling, and not just about us, but for the future, and the past."

There was something about Rocco's presence that made her feel restless, that made her need to move, walk, put a little distance between them. She never felt that way about Marius. For her, Marius had been like a favorite blanket…a warm embrace. She'd melted in his arms, finding such comfort in his nearness. There was none of that with Rocco.

"I can't explain it so that you'd understand." Clare's voice sharpened. "I sometimes don't understand it, but I do feel guilty. I feel guilty that I'm alive and Marius is dead. I feel guilty that Marius died without knowing we'd made a child. I feel guilty that Adriano won't have the loving father he should have. I feel guilty for even having this conversation, considering a future where I'm replacing Marius—"

"You're not replacing Marius," Rocco growled. "Let's agree on that one point. He will never be replaced. He can't be replaced. Clare, we both know Marius is irreplaceable. So that's not what this is about. This is about making sure his son, someone incredibly important, has the best life possible, and I'm not so vain to think that there can't be other men to love him as a father, but I can assure you, that I will love him as a son. As my son. Because he is the closest thing to a son I'll ever have."

"You could have children of your own—"

"No. That's not in the cards." His features hardened, his jaw jutting like granite. Even his silver gaze looked like stone. "It is you, Clare, or it is no one."

His fierce tone felt like a blow to her chest and she took a step back, shocked. Marius avoided conflict but Rocco's words landed with a thump in her chest. His words shocked her, and she didn't know if she was flattered or horrified.

*It is you, Clare, or it is no one.*

The grim certainty in his voice forced her gaze up and she looked into his eyes, trying to see what it was that made him say such things. He didn't want to marry again, but he'd marry her. He didn't want to date again, but he'd been envious of her and Marius's happiness. It didn't make sense, but she did believe Rocco would take his role as a surrogate father to Adriano seriously, and with Adriano wanting Rocco in his life, she was the only thing standing in the way.

"When would we marry?" she asked, voice surprisingly steady.

"As soon as we could get the necessary paperwork. Two weeks? Ten days?"

So soon. She swallowed around the lump in her throat. "I imagine we will get married at a courthouse?"

"That is no wedding."

"I don't need a wedding."

"It's your first marriage, you should have a wedding. I'll have someone handle the details. Is there anything you'd like…anything you don't want?"

She was already second-guessing her decision. "Just simple, please. Simple and quick."

Back at the villa, with Rocco on his way to Rome, Clare locked herself in her bedroom and cried.

What had she done?

Why had she agreed to this?

It was foolish. She'd lost her mind, gotten caught up in the moment trying to make everyone happy. But marriage to Rocco wouldn't make her happy.

It wasn't just that Rocco was still virtually a stranger, but it felt like a betrayal to Marius's memory. How could she move on already? She'd loved him so dearly; she wasn't ready to replace him. She didn't think she could ever replace him. Rocco could say what he wanted, but she didn't really know him, not yet. Yes, they were building a new relationship, but the past weighed heavy. He hadn't been kind to her in the past. He'd been hard and brooding and what if that was the real Rocco?

Marriage was such a huge step and yes, she was doing it for Adriano, but that didn't ease all of her fears. In fact, the fears were so strong that she didn't know how to reconcile her heart and her head.

She needed time. She needed to think this through and not be rushed into a decision.

Clare had other homes, other properties she and Adriano would be safe at. She'd find someplace for them, someplace Rocco couldn't find them, at least not immediately, which would give her time to pull herself together.

Of course she'd send him a message—a text or an email, something. She'd try to explain. She owed him that much at least.

In the morning at breakfast she told Adriano that they were going to go on a trip, fly to the United States, and visit some of the properties she owned.

"To Florida?" he asked, aware that her father lived there.

"I was thinking we'd go to California. We have a big house and vineyard we've never been to. I thought maybe we would go see it and decide if we want to keep it or sell it. You could help me decide."

Adriano hesitated. "Is uncle coming?"

Clare froze, guilt washing through her. "No. I hadn't planned on it. California is far away."

"But he's my uncle."

"And we just spent several days with him. He has work and things he needs to take care of in Rome."

"Maybe we should go to Rome instead."

Her pulse thudded harder. "What would we do in Rome?"

Adriano answered promptly. "*Potremmo andare a vedere piu castelli e rovine.*" *We could go see more castles and ruins.*

"But if we go to California we could maybe go to Disneyland, see Mickey Mouse."

"Then *zio* should come."

"But wouldn't it be more fun if it was just us?" she asked, voice low.

"No. I like my uncle."

Adriano had never been so fixated on anyone or anything before and it was throwing Clare off balance. She could understand Adriano's enthusiasm to a point; their family was very small; it was just the two of them, so the addition of a new relative had to be exciting, but what about Rocco did Adriano like so much? "What is your favorite thing about *zio*?"

Adriano took the question very seriously, taking several long moments to think. Finally he answered. "*Zio* knows many things. He is Italian, and family. My family." His dark head tipped and his gaze met hers. "What do you like?"

Again her pulse felt jagged, beating fast, making her breathless. "That he is your uncle, your family."

"*Our* family." Adriano's small hand gestured from her to him, the gesture so very Latin and expressive.

She smiled and swallowed, trying to hold the tears back. He was such a beautiful bright boy. He deserved the sun and the moon and the stars, and she'd try to give him that and more, but a father wasn't in the picture. Marriage was not in the picture. She needed to break this off quickly, and if Rocco remained in Adriano's life, it would be as an uncle, and nothing more.

Rocco read the letter delivered by courier to him at his office and then set it aside. He walked out onto the penthouse terrace which looked out over the Roman Forum. He loved the columns and ruins, the remnants of older civilizations. Centuries passed and technology changed, but man didn't.

Clare wasn't going to marry him after all.

Rocco's lips twisted. Part of him was angry, but another part felt sympathetic, aware that Clare must be in turmoil. He didn't blame her. Death and grief were impossible things. Grief lingered on and on. Rocco felt as if he spent most of his life in mourning. He didn't even know what it was to not grieve. Grief was always with him. The loss of all of those he loved. So no, any anger he felt wasn't toward Clare, but toward fate, which had made life so difficult.

He understood her note quite well, but it wasn't that simple. He wasn't going to walk away from her, or abandon Adriano. He still wanted to give Adriano the family name. He still wanted Adriano to be raised as a Cosentino.

And then there was Clare. He still wanted Clare. After that kiss, after the fierce physical connection he wanted her more than ever. She was his. She was always meant to be his.

Rocco returned to his desk and after sitting down he made some calls, discovering she'd left the villa for the executive airport. He made another call and her flight plan had been filed, an international flight plan and she'd be taking off within the hour.

He made another call and his helicopter was on

the way. He was heading to the business airport. Rocco was not going to let her go without a fight.

Clare couldn't believe it when Rocco boarded the jet. Her flight had been delayed due to a mechanical— at least that's what she'd been told—but as Rocco walked down the narrow aisle toward her she wondered if that was true.

"Zio!" Adriano cried, delighted to see his uncle.

Rocco put a hand on the top of the boy's head even as his gaze locked with Clare's. "Where are you heading?" he asked her lightly, conversationally.

"California," Adriano answered, tipping his head back to see Rocco better. "I wanted you to come, but Mama said you had to work."

"California?" Rocco said, sitting down in one of the leather chairs that formed a sitting area, two on one side facing two on the other. "What will you do there?"

"Maybe go to Disneyland," Adriano said, unbuckling his seat belt and sliding out of his seat. He went to Rocco and climbed on his lap. "Do you meet Mickey Mouse?"

Clare shifted uncomfortably, aware that Rocco was watching her, his gaze pinning her to her seat. She'd known he would look for her, and suspected he'd find her, but she hadn't expected him to find her so soon, before she'd even left the ground.

Her letter to him was supposed to arrive today, after she'd departed, not before. Clare put a hand to her head, feeling it throb. Nothing was working out the way she wanted. Why?

"Are you well?" Rocco asked, his voice low, his tone surprisingly gentle, but then, Adriano was snuggling on his lap as if they were lifelong friends.

"Are you furious?" She asked, answering his question with a question of her own. She didn't like anger. Her father had been prone to terrible outbursts, rages that made everyone around him cower. It had been a relief to move to Europe, away from the rage and outbursts from a man who enjoyed his own temper tantrums.

"Not furious, and not upset, just sorry you felt it necessary to run away from me. Rather than a note, I wish you would have talked to me. Wish you could have talked to me," he corrected.

Clare swallowed and glanced out the window to the tarmac. "I didn't know what to say." She looked back at him. "It seemed an easier thing to write, less emotion, less drama—"

"I'd argue that running away has a certain element of drama to it."

His tone was mild, and amused, and Clare blushed because there were other reasons she'd run away, reasons she couldn't admit. Rocco exerted such a strange power over her. She didn't want to be drawn to him, didn't want the attraction and curiosity, but when near him, her body overrode her head. She wanted to be strong, wanted to resist him and the only way she could do that was if there was distance between them.

If he didn't come for her.

If he didn't fight for her.

"Do you really want to go to California?" he asked, black eyebrow lifting.

"No," Adriano said firmly. He leaned forward and looked his mother in the eye. "We want to stay here with Zio Rocco."

# CHAPTER SEVEN

EVERYTHING WAS HAPPENING quickly now, too quickly. Clare's head spun. She wanted to slow time down, wanted to slow Rocco down, but now that she'd agreed to marry him, he'd put the wheels in motion, and they were turning. Spinning.

The late September weather was perfect for a wedding, not that there would be guests who had to worry about traveling to attend a wedding. It would just be the family and the staff, but still, a wedding deserved a blue sky and sunshine.

The wedding was to be held in the Cosentino family's chapel at the family's ancestral home, a historic palazzo, in Rome. The chapel had been decorated with garlands of flowers, pale pink and dark pink roses with delicate orchids. Clare had left all of the wedding plans to Rocco's assistant, as she couldn't bring herself to plan another wedding, especially one which would see her become a Cosentino, just not the right wife to the right Cosentino. But for the sake of

Adriano they'd agreed to make it picture-perfect, and so it was a grand wedding on a very intimate scale.

Her wedding gown was the palest pink. Just as she couldn't bring herself to plan another wedding, Clare couldn't bring herself to wear white, not after having a son, not after burying her love. Instead of a traditional white dress, she wore a stunning couture gown with a full chiffon skirt and a fitted bodice with the most delicate cap sleeves. In the soft pink gown she felt as if she were a butterfly about to fly away. If only she could fly away.

Even though the wedding ceremony was small, it was a proper ceremony, and long, at least to Clare it seemed long, and she felt faint at one point, the warmth in the chapel and the fragrant flowers making her dizzy.

She'd glanced at Adriano who stood next to Rocco, and sternly she reminded herself that this was for him. Adriano would be protected. He'd have two of them to watch out for him, and two of them to love him, and should life become difficult, two to fight for him.

But then her eyes met Rocco's silver gaze and she couldn't breathe. It was too much, too quickly. Her mouth dried and her lips parted and she wanted to run away, run—

Rocco reached out, putting a hand on her lower back. "Are you okay?"

She shook her head, tears filling her eyes.

He held up a hand to the priest, halting him mid-sentence, midservice. "You don't have to do this," Rocco said quietly, supporting her weight as her legs were trembling like mad. "We can stop this right now."

She couldn't look away from his eyes. She could see his concern, and feel it, too. "Do you mean that?" she answered huskily.

"Absolutely. I want to marry you, if it's what you want to do. But if it's not, we stop and just let it go."

Clare glanced down at Adriano waiting so patiently at Rocco's side. Clare might not love Rocco, but Adriano did. She couldn't disappoint her son, not when he was so happy to have found family. And truthfully, this wasn't even about love anymore. There were so many other emotions, so many other conflicting feelings...desire, fear, attraction and more.

She craved things she couldn't articulate, craved power and pressure, heat and sensation. She wanted to be wanted. She wanted to be touched. She wanted to be seduced. But it was also rather terrifying as she'd never felt these intense needs and wants with Marius. Marius never made her ache...or crave.

"It's just warm in here," she said, pushing away the thoughts, refusing to feel guilty for wanting something she'd never known, wanting heat to make her melt and burn. "I'm fine." Her voice shook and she added more firmly, "I'll be fine, I promise. Let's continue, please."

Twenty minutes later the ceremony was over

and the photographer posed them, requesting they stand with the priest, then with the witnesses who were Ava and Gio, and then it was the three of them, Rocco, Clare and Adriano, and finally, it was just her and Rocco.

She swallowed around the lump in her throat as he faced her, both her hands in his, and looked down into her eyes. He didn't smile, even though the photographer kept trying to get a smile from them. But his gaze wasn't icy. She didn't know what was in his eyes, only there was no ice, and nothing cruel. Determination, yes. Pride, yes. Possession, possibly? It crossed her mind that he was glad she'd become his wife—

Adriano suddenly flung himself at Clare's legs, laughing as he escaped Ava's hand that had been trying to keep him in place.

Rocco laughed, too, and lifted Adriano up into his arms. "Let's go inside. We're having an early dinner tonight so we can all celebrate together."

They had dinner in a room painted silver and gold. Pink flowers with silver- and gold-painted leaves formed a centerpiece, and the china was white with gold, and the glasses were pink Venetian stemware. It was just the three of them eating in the formal dining room. Adriano was curious about everything and took in the new environment with admirable calm and confidence. The meal, five courses' worth, did drag on, far more food than Clare wanted or needed, but finally a wedding cake was served and Adriano, sleepy and yawning, tried to wake up enough to eat a slice.

He managed to eat three and a half bites before his eyes began to close again. Clare had taken her watch off for the wedding and couldn't alert Ava, but someone must have because it was just a few minutes later that Ava appeared, her gaze meeting Clare's.

Clare nodded, and Ava lifted him from his chair. He nestled his chest on her shoulder and closed his eyes.

"I'll be just down the hall," Clare whispered to Ava.

"I'll be in the nursery with him. Gio is here, too, don't worry."

As Ava passed by Rocco, Rocco reached out and smoothed Adriano's dark hair. The tender gesture made Clare's heart tighten and her eyes burn.

But she wasn't going to fall apart, she told herself. There would be no tears tonight. She'd made the decision to marry and she was now Rocco's wife, and there would be no more looking back, no more lamenting the past.

Rocco sat at the end of the table feeling Clare's emotion. He was always aware of her, but tonight he could see the shimmer of tears in her eyes and he remembered how she'd trembled in his arm in the chapel, exhausted, overwhelmed, uncertain of her decision. But then she'd found her resolve and she'd made it through the ceremony and they'd made it through the dinner, too.

This was not a happy wedding, this wasn't one of those events celebrated by a loving family and dozens of friends. They had no others. No one to celebrate with, no one who'd care that this wasn't a love match…at least on Clare's part.

Rocco had no regrets, though. This was what he'd wanted. He'd wanted her for so long, and he'd waited for her, not allowing another woman into his life, unwilling to even entertain the idea of another woman for him. He'd loved his wife, and he'd loved Clare and that was all. There would be no other loves, not for him.

But he hated seeing Clare with tears in her eyes, hated knowing she was struggling. He wasn't struggling. He had what he wanted. Clare as his woman, his wife. It might take weeks, maybe months, but one day she'd drop her guard and let him in. Not just tolerate him but love him. Which is why he could be patient. He'd waited this long for her…what was another six months, or a year?

He'd give her time, and seduce her so slowly she wouldn't even realize she was being wooed, and won.

They had separate bedrooms, a his and her layout with an enormous shared dressing room in the middle. Alone in her room Clare couldn't get out of her wedding gown, not without help and unlike at her villa, she had no staff here to call, no one available to help her with the hooks that lined the hidden seams of the dress. She could ask Ava to come to her, but that wasn't Ava's job, and Clare respected the nanny too much to ask her to leave her room just to help Clare undress. On her wedding night. It would look silly and possibly cause gossip that she didn't need.

Drawing a breath for courage, Clare went to the door between her and Rocco's room. She knocked once, firmly, and waited.

He opened the door after a few moments, so tall and broad shouldered that he filled the doorway, nearly blocking all the light shining behind him. He was in the process of undressing, and his white shirt was unbuttoned, but he was still wearing his black trousers. His chest, although scarred, was a wonder of hard muscle, planes and hollows and a dusting of black hair low on his abdomen, disappearing into his trousers. She jerked her head up and focused on his chin—so much safer than his hips, or even his eyes or mouth. "I'm afraid I need assistance with my dress. There are dozens of little hooks."

"I was wondering if you'd need help," he said. "But I didn't want to presume."

"These gowns are made for women with stylists and designers," she said, trying to sound casual when her pulse raced and her mouth felt dry.

"Or husbands," he said lightly, gesturing for her to step back. She did and he followed her into her room.

He took a seat in one of the armchairs in front

of the marble surround and reached a hand to her.
"Come. Where are these hooks?"

She stood with her back to him. "They're tucked
into those small seams. I warn you, there are many."

"I am prepared to do my duty," he said dryly,
hands settling on her hips, his warmth steeling
through her skirts into her skin.

She could feel his fingers on her back exploring
the dress and the exquisite tailoring and held her
breath as he slowed to inspect the long seam where
the majority of the hooks were. With one hand on
her lower back to keep her steady he unfastened the
first hook, and then the next. Clare closed her eyes
trying not to let her imagination run wild, but every
time his knuckles brushed her spine, every time her
gown opened a little more, shivers raced through
her, little darts of sensation that made her mouth
dry and heart race.

She'd never been undressed by anyone before.
It was new and erotic and she didn't want it to be
erotic. She wanted to think of Rocco as a partner,
not a lover, but his touch stirred her senses and as
her gown opened down the back, revealing bare skin
she found herself wishing he'd touch her, slide a finger across her sensitive skin, caress the hollows of
her lower back.

Her inner muscles clenched as he turned her side-
ways to work the last of the hooks that ran on the
seam beneath the corset-like bodice. His fingers

brushed the underside of her breast and she bit into her lip, feeling carnal and full of longing.

It had been so long since she'd been loved. It had been years since she'd been held and touched. If Rocco wanted to kiss her, she'd let him. If he wanted to take her to bed, she'd welcome the company. She hated feeling so much need, but standing half-naked in front of him had filled her with wants and needs that felt almost overwhelming.

The bodice of her gown slid down to her hips, and then Rocco's hands were at her hips helping to ease the gown over her bottom, sliding it down until the pale pink gown pooled at her feet.

She turned to face him, her hands covering her breasts, her eyes meeting his.

His gaze traveled over her, from her dark hair over her covered breasts to her rounded hips and the delicate pink scrap of satin that was her thong.

"You're beautiful," he said, his deep voice pitched low, the husky timber reverberating in her.

"I want you," he added, reaching out to capture a curled tendril that rested on her collarbone, the warmth of his fingers setting her skin on fire, "but I can't make love to you tonight, and I won't make love to you until you're comfortable being…mine."

"I am," she said faintly, face hot.

He put his hand on her waist, stroked her side, and her gently rounded hip. It was, oh, so delicious, she thought, and so seductive. Clare swayed a little as he plucked at the tiny thong, adjusting the pink fabric to better cover her. She sucked in a breath as her nerves screamed with pleasure. He was toying with her, she thought, and her body loved it. He ran his palm over her bottom, cupping the full cheek, caressing on one side, and then the other before taking his hand away.

"You're not," he said, looking up into her face. "You can hardly look at me. One day when you're ready, we will make love, but not until then."

Disappointment rushed through her as he rose and stepped around her. She felt silly and naked, and rather rejected. "Lots of people have sex on the first date. This isn't even a first date. We're married—"

"And I don't want to have sex with you. I want more than that. I want it, when we come together, to mean something." He tipped her chin up and looked deeply into her eyes. "Trust me, we will be glad we waited—"

"I doubt it," she interrupted, cheeks hot, knees locking, her innermost core clenching. "I think you just enjoy having all the control!"

He drew her into his arms and kissed her then, a hot fierce kiss of possession that stole her breath and fogged her brain. She couldn't think of anything but him, her senses overcome, her bare body pressed to his frame. He was so warm and his arms wrapped around her, drawing her closer, his hands cupping her butt, and lifting her up against him so that she felt the length of his erection through the trousers, his body hard against her pelvis. His body so much muscle and power.

By the time he let her go, she didn't know where she was, only that everything within her was hot and molten. She couldn't bear for him to leave her like this, couldn't bear to be left so full of unanswered desire.

But then he brushed her cheek, the pad of his thumb stroking her swollen lower lip before heading to the door where he quietly wished her a good night and disappeared into the connecting dressing room, his door closing behind him.

Rocco took the longest, coldest shower of his life, and he emerged still hard, still throbbing, still so hungry for her.

She was beautiful, truly beautiful and the shape of her, and the softness of her skin, and the tiny little moans she made while he touched her nearly drove him mad. All he wanted was to be in her body, feeling her warmth and softness, giving her the pleasure and release they both knew she wanted. That he wanted, too, but his needs came second to hers. And he'd been waiting five years for her and now that she was his wife, he didn't just want her body, he wanted her heart.

Clare didn't understand this new marriage, or her new husband, who was as handsome and charming and devoted as a new husband could be…except that he avoided touching her, and kept kisses to a minimum, mostly a light kiss good-night before they retired to their own rooms.

They didn't sleep together once that first week.

Rocco was attentive during the day, spending time with her and Adriano. He planned excursions for them, making the honeymoon feel like a holiday, one that focused on Adriano, which she appreciated, but Clare wanted Rocco to focus on her.

Instead they enjoyed a private tour of the coliseum, Rocco arranging for them to enter an hour before it opened to the public so their tour was truly private, focused on the interests of a young child, featuring tales of brave gladiators and wild beasts, a moveable stage, and how it would have looked filled with all the people.

Another day they visited the Trevi Fountain and the Spanish Stairs, this done under a very tight, discreet, security detail. There was also a trip to the mountains, where they did an easy hike in the regional park of the Monti Simbruini, walking amongst the birch trees, keeping their eyes open for wildlife. Adriano was thrilled to spot a peregrine falcon, although he'd called it a hawk, and Rocco saw a fox peeking between ferns and rocks while Clare mostly saw gophers. They enjoyed a lunch at a guesthouse that had been booked for them. The service was attentive, and the meal was delicious. Clare had no reason to complain. Not with the guesthouse anyway.

Now, Rocco…he wasn't just puzzling, he was infuriating.

He was charming during the day, but he wasn't oblivious to her. She knew he watched her, and his focus was intense; his focus made her feel naked, breathless. He wanted her. She could feel how he desired her. But why then at night did he stay away?

Why kiss her good-night and then disappear, leaving her to go to bed alone?

She'd been alone for years now. She shouldn't mind, but she did.

Another day passed. Another day of a devoted husband being attentive to his new family. Another night where he slipped away from her after a sweet, chaste kiss and a pleasant good-night.

The chaste kiss made her rage, and she knew he felt her impatience. Annoyance. She knew because the energy between them just kept building, the energy humming strongly, the awareness so hot and sharp the air practically crackled with desire. And still Rocco left her.

Two weeks of marriage with no intimacy. No husband in her bed. No touch, no friction, no satisfaction.

Clare was beyond frustrated. She was ready for more from her husband, certainly more than conversation and little pecks good-night. The next time he kissed her good-night, she wouldn't let him walk away from her. She'd demand more. He owed her more. They were married, weren't they?

The next time was that very evening, after dinner, after drinks in his gorgeous library that also served as a media room with an enormous TV screen that came down, hiding a long wall of books. The sur-

round sound system had been built into the antique
shelves giving the old room new life and purpose.
After Adriano had gone to bed they'd curled up on
the leather sofa and watched a thriller, and it had
been quite intense in places, resulting in Clare sitting ever closer to Rocco.

Even though they were both watching the film,
and she was trying to concentrate on the plot, she
was more aware of Rocco, and his arm behind her
shoulder, his other hand on her thigh.

At first the hand on her thigh was nothing, but
gradually his palm felt warmer, and she grew hotter, and she didn't know if she shifted, or his hand
moved up, but his fingers were on the inside of her
thigh and he wasn't doing anything, but the weight
of his hand and the pressure made her wish he'd do
something.

The movie finally ended and Rocco turned off the
TV with a remote, and then pushed another button
on the remote and the screen disappeared.

"Did you enjoy that?" he asked, turning to look
at her.

"I did."

His hand, still between her thighs, moved up several inches. "You seemed distracted."

She met his silver gaze and it wasn't innocent. A
knowing heat glowed in his eyes and his hand inched
higher again, his fingers so close to the juncture of
her thighs.

"It's hard to concentrate when your husband's hand is making you melt."

"You do feel hot," he agreed, his hand now against the seam of her leggings, right where she wanted him.

"I think you should kiss me," she said huskily.

"I've been thinking the same thing." Rocco lifted her up and settled her on his lap so that she was facing him. His lap was warm, and hard, and she could feel him through her thin leggings. She shuddered a little at the erotic pressure of his body against her.

His hands were on her hips, holding her firmly, fingers grazing her hipbones making her gasp at how sensitive he made her feel. His touch lit fire everywhere beneath her skin, and she tried not to wiggle because every little movement made his shaft rub her there where she had a million nerve endings. But then when his hands cupped her butt, holding her in such a way that she felt open, Clare whimpered. "I thought you were going to kiss me."

"Don't worry, I am. I just want to feel you first. You have such a beautiful shape, all curves and softness. I could sink into your softness."

"I wish you would," she answered.

He clasped her face, his mouth covering hers and he kissed her then, a deep, fierce, intoxicating kiss, a kiss of barely leashed hunger, a kiss that promised endless pleasure. She wanted endless pleasure. She wanted him with her and in her, wanted to be as close as possible. He held her hips to his, and as he kissed her, she could feel him grow harder, and harder, until they were both throbbing with need.

She wrapped her arms around his neck, pressing her breasts to his chest, craving friction and satisfaction.

When he broke off the kiss she was certain he was going to suggest going to his room, or hers and she wanted it, was ready for it, but instead he gazed down into her eyes. "I shouldn't have let this happen. I got carried away. I'm sorry."

She stiffened, caught off guard, the apology a blow to her chest, making her heart seize up and the air bottle in her lungs. She hated the apology, and found herself—unreasonably, perhaps—hating him.

How could he say such a thing when her mouth was still tender, the lower lip tingling, her body filled with shivery sensation? How could he apologize for any of it? "It was just a kiss," she said lowly, climbing off his lap and tugging on her tunic, covering her hips and bottom, adjusting the sleeves. "Nothing to apologize for," she added, looking anywhere but at him. "And certainly nothing to feel guilty about."

"I don't feel guilty. You're my wife." He reached for her hand, tugged her back so that she had to face him. His gaze was like molten silver, hot, so hot, but his expression as fierce, determined. "You're the one I'm trying to protect. I don't want *you* to feel guilty…later."

She tried to shake him off, but he wouldn't let go. "And you think I would."

"I know you would. You love him. Not me."

Clare flinched, stunned. So that's what this was about. Oh, wow. She hadn't expected that, but maybe she should have. Ironically, Clare certainly hadn't been thinking of Marius. She thought of him less and less lately, but she'd thought maybe it was a good thing, maybe it meant she was ready to move forward and live again.

"I married you," she said, hating the lump in her throat. "I chose to say yes. I chose to start a life with you."

"I worry I've rushed you."

Clare didn't love him, if that's what he wanted. She didn't know if she'd ever love him, but she was attracted to him and desired him. These past few nights she'd touched herself trying to be patient, but it was him she wanted, and the pleasure his powerful body promised. She wanted all of it—the discovery, the release, the comfort. "Many people fall in bed on the first date. We've been married for two weeks now and there have only been these little kisses, and that's fine for children, but we're adults, and married. Is there a reason I can't desire you?" she asked, chin lifting defiantly. "You are my husband. You are now mine."

The corner of his mouth tilted up slightly even as her words made his expression fiercer. He pulled her down onto the leather sofa and stretched out over her, his body trapping her on the couch. He kissed her deeply, possessively, his tongue tasting her, teasing her, a hand beneath her bottom, holding her to him.

This is what she'd wanted, this fire, this burn, hot wine in her veins, heat and need between her legs.

She thought she'd go mad with need. And in that moment, with him close, but not close enough, Clare thought she'd do—give—anything to have him in her, filling her, making her feel complete. Because she'd been empty and lonely, and she'd had enough. Enough chivalry.

Enough safety. Enough being smart and careful and good.

"I want you," she breathed against his mouth. "It's not him. It's you, only you."

His gaze locked with hers. Her heart pounded, thudding painfully in her chest.

"When you kiss me," she continued, "I know it's you kissing me. When you touch me, I know it's you touching me. I am not pretending you are someone else. I am not fantasizing about anyone else. I am with you, and only you."

He captured her hands and lifted them over her head, holding them captive in one hand even as he slid a thigh between hers, his knee where she was hot and wet. "When I see you," he rasped, his head bending to press a light kiss beneath her ear to the side of her neck. "I only see you. I only desire you."

He transferred her hands to one of his and allowed the other hand to slide down her body, from her breasts over her flat stomach to the hem of her tunic. He reached beneath the tunic to stroke up one thigh, and then down her thigh and then back up again, his touch slow, building the pleasure but also the torment. Finally he was at the elastic waistband of her leggings and he tugged it down on her hips, low, lower. With her tunic pushed up, and her leggings down, she was exposed, the only thing between her and his eyes her orange silk thong, which offered little coverage and even less protection.

He pressed his palm to the orange silk covering her mound, and when she shuddered, he lowered his head and kissed her there, through the damp silk.

She gasped, legs trembling. He was touching her now beneath the silk, ever so gently, fingers slipping through her curls to her very tender skin, and she nearly cried at the exquisite sensation. "You're wet," he said.

"You're a very good kisser."

"That's all from a kiss?"

"Do you want a medal, Rocco?"

He laughed softly, amused, and aroused. She heard it in the huskiness of his voice, and the gleam in his eyes. He was still lightly stroking, exploring, watching her face and she tried not to squirm, so difficult when she ached for him.

With his mouth on her, blowing on her through the silk, his hand was between her thighs, circling the tender inner lips, outlining the shape of her, making her gasp and tilt her hips trying to capture more.

He gave her more, thrusting a finger inside her and she rocked against his hand to feel more pleasure.

The tip of his tongue was against her nub and his finger found a spot within her that craved pressure and friction. She panted as he plunged another finger into her, taking her, filling her, then retreating to do it again, slow and deep, while he sucked on her silk-covered clit, pleasure building, pressure everywhere, his mouth and tongue and teeth driving her over the edge. She wrestled her hands free and one hand pushed hard against his shoulder while the other tangled in his hair. Clare cried his name as she shattered, the intensity of the orgasm rippling through her, again and then again.

When she'd finally begun to recover and pull what was left of her blown mind together, she looked at Rocco who was watching her, and waiting for her to return to the present.

"That was…uh…um…amazing," she said, cheeks still hot and flushed.

"That was just the *cicchetti*," he murmured, cicchetti meaning small snack. "Wait until I give you everything."

Upstairs Rocco took her to his room, and she slept with him there, safe in the circle of his muscular arm, his broad chest against her back.

He woke her up in the night and made love to her slowly, thoroughly, and Clare didn't think she'd ever understood the power of sex until then. Of making love. It was so deeply satisfying that it wasn't just a physical act, but emotional, almost spiritual. With him in her, she felt whole, and at peace. Grateful, she wrapped her arms around his shoulders and held him tightly, loving the press of his hard chest to her breasts, his hips against hers, legs tangled. They'd become one, and she didn't want it to end. She wanted to feel this connected forever, and kissing him back, she gave herself up to him, and in doing so, Clare felt a shift within her, as though a lock had been turned and her chest opened, her heart freed.

For the first time since the wedding she thought—knew—she could be happy with him. That they could be happy together.

Maybe, maybe this was what was meant to be.

The next morning they breakfasted with Adriano and over breakfast Rocco asked Adriano what his favorite beach was.

Adriano thought and then answered. "I only know the beach at our villa." He thought for another moment. "But Castello di Palo has a beach, too."

"What about a beach with palm trees? And water so warm you never want to get out of it?" Rocco's eyebrow rose. "And sand so soft it's like touching velvet?"

Adriano's eyes grew wide and he glanced at his mom, who was looking at Rocco with a little amusement and puzzlement. Where was Rocco going with this?

Rocco looked at her, creases at his eyes, the smile

lines making him even more attractive. "Should we go somewhere? Have a proper honeymoon—taking Adriano, of course."

Clare hadn't felt deprived in any way. Going on a honeymoon hadn't even crossed her mind, not when they'd married for the sake of Adriano, but also, taking a holiday, going somewhere tropical and exotic…exposing Adriano to someplace new. Her pulse jumped. Excitement flooded her. "I'd love that," she answered. "When could we go?"

"How soon can you be ready?"

"An hour. Maybe two so I won't feel frantic."

"Take your time, but remember, you won't need too much. It's an island and we'll be living in swimsuits much of the time."

They left from the private executive airport outside Rome, traveling in one of Rocco's private jets which would be able to land on a shorter runway, which was the only runway on the island. Ava and Gio were coming, too, which made Clare feel better as she knew little about where they were going, but was also excited to just be surprised. For years she'd been in charge of everything, having to think of everything, responsible for every detail, worried that she might make a potentially tragic mistake. But Clare trusted Rocco. She knew he'd protect them and take care of them and she could let go and just breathe. And be.

They landed on a tiny island in the middle of turquoise water. Clare had held her breath as the pilots made the most of the short runway, coming to a quick but smooth stop. Beyond the window were palm trees and the sparkling ocean. Rocco had been holding Adriano on his lap for the descent and Adriano's gaze was fixed on the view. "Are we here, Zio?" he asked.

"We are here," Rocco said. "And it's going to be so warm outside. You'll think it's a little bit like heaven."

It was more than a little like heaven, Clare thought, as they transferred into little golf carts with Rocco at the wheel of one, and Gio and Ava and the luggage in the other. The drive was lined with trees and blooming shrubs, flowers she recognized from growing up in southern Florida—hibiscus, plumeria, orchids, jasmine and ginger. Close to the house tangerine cannas with dark green and purple leaves competed for attention with purple and pink bougainvillea. The house itself was a sprawling compound of cool white stucco walls and enormous glass windows and doors that could be opened all the way so that living flowed seamlessly between inside the house and outside.

Adriano ran through the house, all built on one level, and every room with breathtaking views. Furniture was low and welcoming, the fabric all neutrals so nothing competed with the vivid colors of paradise.

Rocco walked Adriano and Clare through the garden, on paths, and off, explaining to Adriano that he was not to go near a pool or fountain without an adult, and that if he wanted to go for a swim, he only had to ask and he'd be taken to the beach or the pool. He crouched down in front of the boy, hands on his shoulders. "Your mama loves you and we must not make her worry. When we love people, we take care of them, yes?"

Adriano nodded somberly. "*Sì.*"

"Good." Rocco kissed his forehead then added, "Remember, family always takes care of each other, and you are a Cosentino."

Adriano looked even more serious and nodded again.

Rocco rose and they finished their tour of the gardens but Clare found herself replaying Rocco's words. *Family always takes care of each other.*

And they were family. Rocco and Clare and Adriano.

She'd become a Cosentino at last, even though it hadn't been the way any of them had expected, but Marius would approve. He'd be glad that Rocco was there with them, for them, glad that Rocco had stepped up when Clare and Adriano were on their own.

Making love with Rocco was better than good. It answered a need that she hadn't even known existed, healing the broken pieces of her. Rocco's body, crisscrossed with scars, echoed the scars she carried on her heart, scars she'd had since a child whose world had been upended when her parents had gone through a terrible divorce, and then her mother's death, followed by an exile to Europe where she wouldn't be in the way anymore. Rocco made love to her as if she were perfect and beautiful, and in his arms, she became almost perfect and beautiful. The hollow aching sensation in her was filling and fading. She slept better, she ate better, she felt better about everything, including the future.

Especially the future.

Before they made love, Clare had thought it would take them weeks to become comfortable with each other, that intimacy might feel awkward at times, and that they'd probably leave the heat of the bedroom in the bedroom and function like colleagues out of it.

She was wrong. Rocco was sensual and sexual night and day. She felt him even when they weren't in the same room and the connection was intense, and constant, the desire always there.

It was almost like being born again, born into this different body, born into this new life. Clare had never cared that much about sex. She'd enjoyed it, but it hadn't been earth-shattering, not in the way making love with Rocco was shattering. With Rocco it was such a fierce, physical coupling that afterward she felt raw and naked and, oh, so very vulnerable. But Rocco always held her, and reassured her that she was the most glorious thing in the world, and he made her believe it. Made her believe she was safe. She'd hired Gio to keep her and her son safe, but he was hired, he was paid to protect. Rocco vowed to protect her with his life.

And she knew he would.

In a matter of weeks she'd come to trust him in a way she'd never trusted anyone.

With Rocco she felt safe to explore her boundaries, safe to feel everything, and when something was too much, she could tell him and he never questioned her, or pressured her, or made her doubt herself in any way.

It was amazing how they'd married for Adriano and yet the marriage was proving to be her salvation. She would have never dreamed that Rocco could be so patient and good with her, or so loving and devoted to her. Time and again he went out of his way to please her, and pleasure her, and also give her space to process emotion her way.

With time, she could be happy with him. Very happy. As happy and content as if it had been a love match.

Everything on the island was easy; life was easy, the days relaxed. Neither Clare nor Rocco were at computers or taking phone calls. They'd both agreed to unplug from the world and put business on hold. It was a much-needed break, one that Rocco was grateful for as it gave him time to just relax and be with Clare and Adriano. Being with them, both of them, felt right, and normal. The three of them were a family, his family.

Rocco could see Marius in Adriano, but he could also see Clare. Adriano was very smart, as well as perceptive, and Rocco looked forward to their morning walk each day, going out after breakfast just the two of them to walk on the beach and see if they could find shells and look for fish swimming in the shallow water near the beach.

It was during this time that Rocco would tell Adriano about his father, Marius, and how good and loving he'd been, a friend to many, and a wonderful much loved younger brother. One day on their walk, as they bent over to look at a little crab digging down into the sand, Adriano asked if he would be a brother.

"Do you want to be a brother?" Rocco asked him.

"Yes," Adriano answered. "A brother like you. The big brother."

Rocco's chest squeezed, too aware that he had failed his brother, that Adriano should aspire to more. Rocco knew he was no hero. "You want to be like your papa," Rocco said. "Your papa was the best man I knew."

Adriano began walking again. "But I want to be like you," he said after a minute. "My new papa." He glanced up at Rocco, eyes squinting against the sun. "Papa Rocco."

Nothing more was said, but later during dinner, Adriano called Rocco Papa during the meal and he heard Clare inhale, and saw her expression. She was surprised, but didn't seem angry. Curious more than anything.

"I am your *zio*," Rocco gently corrected.

"And my papa." Adriano gestured across the table. "Papa and Mama."

Rocco opened his mouth to protest, but Clare put a hand on his arm. "It's okay," she said softly. "You are his father now. It's why we married."

"I don't want him to forget his real father," Rocco answered as quietly, deeply conflicted because he loved Adriano and he'd raise Adriano as his son, but at the same time, the only reason Rocco was here was because Marius was gone.

Clare's gaze met his and held. "You are his real father now. No matter what happens, you have made a commitment to him. A commitment to us." Her hand was still on his arm, and she slid her fingers over the back of his wrist, to take his hand in hers. "I've searched my heart and I truly believe Marius wouldn't mind."

That evening as Clare lay in the circle of Rocco's arm, she thought about the conversation at dinner, both Rocco's reluctance to take Marius's place, as well as Adriano's eagerness to have his own papa. It was complicated but not, as they were all so comfortable and happy together.

Clare loved to watch Rocco and Adriano together. If they were walking a great distance, Rocco would swing Adriano onto his shoulders and carry him. Other times he'd walk holding Adriano's small hand. At the end of the day when Adriano was tired, Rocco would carry the child and Adriano would slump against Rocco's chest, sleepy and safe.

They looked like father and son, but of course she never forgot Marius, and she'd talk to him sometimes and thank him. She'd tell him they were doing well and that Adriano was happier than she'd ever known him.

Ever since Adriano's birth, she'd tried to be both mother and father to Adriano, and there were times she thought she was succeeding, but whenever she saw Rocco hug Adriano, or crouch down to talk to him, or help him with something whether it was big or small, she felt Adriano's gratitude, and could see how his big brown eyes would shine.

Adriano's happiness gave her peace. She'd struggled making the decision to marry, but she was glad she'd chosen to give Adriano a father, and not just any father, but Rocco Cosentino, a man of integrity and strength. Rocco was a family man and he'd spent his life putting others first, including Marius. Could there be a better role model for her young son?

They had one more week on the island and then they'd return to Italy. Clare and Rocco spent several evenings discussing which home should be the family home. Rocco suggested the seaside villa because it was outside the city and there was little noise and traffic, but Clare knew Rocco had an office, a large office, and unlike her, he went to the office daily whereas she worked remotely, meeting with staff when necessary, preferring to hold most meetings online.

"Don't you want to raise Adriano in the Cosentino family home? It's where you were raised, and where you raised Marius after your parents died." Clare curled her legs under her, very comfortable in the chair in the living room, the sliding glass doors open so they could enjoy the warm night.

"But it's not really a home," Rocco said after a moment, "not the way you think of a home. It's huge, and so formal. It's easy to feel lost in such a place. It's why I've taken up residence in just one small part of the palazzo. That way I don't have to deal with the rest of it."

"It is a palazzo, but it is also where generations of Cosentinos have lived. I think it's important for Adriano to know his past."

Rocco shrugged uneasily. "Sometimes we can live too much in the past. Sometimes what we need is a break with the past—"

"Rocco! What are you saying?" She turned to look at him more closely. "Your past has made you who you are. You should be proud of your family. You come from a very close, loving family. I envy those family ties, and that commitment to each other. I've never had that. It was one of the things that drew me to Marius. His love of family. His love for you."

Rocco's brow creased. "Sometimes I worry that you've put me on a pedestal. You shouldn't. Don't forget that I once was cold and harsh—"

She laughed, interrupting him, and left her chair to settle into his lap. She put an arm around his shoulder and kissed him lightly, but the moment their lips touched, it was fire, the kiss becoming hot and explosive. Rocco's hand slid under her blouse, under her lace bra to cup her breast, her nipple hardening against his palm. She gasped as he rubbed the tender nipple, her body instantly growing hot, her core tightening, body aching, wanting him, always wanting him.

"I don't recognize that man," she whispered against his mouth as Rocco caressed her, turning her on. He was always turning her on and then giving her pleasure.

Making her feel good, making her happy.

She couldn't imagine being happier.

He carried her into the bedroom and stripping her clothes off, he licked and sucked between her legs until she was panting and squirming, drawing out the pleasure as long as he could, and she felt like clay in Rocco's hands, she was his to love, his to pleasure, and he gave her such pleasure, bringing her to a climax so intense she cried out, shattering in the stars, becoming nothing more than diamond dust.

Later they made love slowly, and it was extraordinary the connection between them. If Clare hadn't known better she would have thought they were made for each other. They came together so well, and satisfied each other so completely, that she felt gratitude and love—

Love.

Clare froze, startled by the realization that yes, she was falling in love with him and no, this wasn't just a physical thing. She enjoyed making love with Rocco, but their relationship had become important to her; he'd become important. Rocco had found his way into her heart, and he'd taken up residence there.

She didn't know how he'd done it. Initially she hadn't wanted him, or needed him, but with time and patience and endless affection he'd melted her reserve and made her care. He'd made her love *him*.

## CHAPTER EIGHT

THEY WERE BACK in Italy and they'd come to a compromise on where they'd live. During the week they'd be at the Cosentino palazzo and on weekends they'd go to her villa where they could relax.

It was a good compromise, Clare thought, and she was the one who'd thought of it. Rocco had been gratified that she'd want to move into his home, and to help her ease the transition, he'd had a suite prepared for her, one that would be fresh and bright with the latest in technology so she could accomplish everything she needed, or wanted, to do while at the palazzo.

The children's nursery was on one of the upper levels of the palazzo, far from the wing where Rocco and Clare were most comfortable, and without even needing to discuss it, Rocco created a comfortable bedroom and playroom for Adriano—airy, colorful rooms sandwiched between the master bedroom suite and Clare's new office suite.

Under Gio's direction, Rocco had also upgraded

palazzo security, adding in cameras and sensors, as well as other essential changes Gio thought necessary. All in all, life in their small portion of the palazzo was comfortable, provided they weren't wandering through the rest of the enormous palazzo itself which had over thirty rooms all shrouded with sheets and covers to protect furniture, a vast ballroom with six Venetian chandeliers, and four hundred years of antiques and family portraits and mementos.

Rocco's personal style favored a clean, modern design so Clare understood why he found the palazzo repressive, but at the same time, she was fascinated by the Cosentinos' history, a history that wove together families and industries, making the Cosentinos powerful for hundreds of years.

Rocco rarely referenced the past, or any of his ancestors, focusing instead on the present and creating new memories for them. He was incredibly thoughtful, always trying to think of activities Adriano would enjoy, as well as romantic moments for just the two of them.

When Clare thought back to her first impressions of him, that he was hard and cold and unfeeling, she smiled, amused, because Rocco was warmth and passion, loyalty and devotion, and it amazed her now that she'd ever thought him so icy and harsh. And maybe Rocco could still be hard with the rest of the world, but he was impossibly gentle with her. He was nothing but thoughtful and patient, and kind. So kind. She and Adriano were lucky to have such a good man in their lives after all the grief and loss. She counted her blessings, aware that Rocco was a gift, a gift that she and Adriano loved without reservation.

Clare told him that night, in between slow, hot, intoxicating kisses. Adriano had been in bed for hours and she and Rocco had made love and then left their bed to get a snack from the kitchen, and they sat with their cheese and chocolate talking and talking and then he leaned over and kissed her, and they returned to the bedroom to continue there.

She didn't want to make love again without him knowing. She didn't want the pleasure to be just a physical thing. He should know how she felt in her heart, in her mind, in her body and soul. "I love you," she whispered, lightly stroking his cheekbone, where he was scarred, where he'd once hurt so much. "You are our knight in shining armor, our hero and our heart."

He looked at her in the dim light of the bedroom and his jaw worked. "I don't deserve that," he said unsteadily, his deep voice a rumble.

"But you do," she said, kissing his lips, and then again. "You have made us all so very happy. I am beyond grateful. I am yours forever."

*I am yours forever.*

The words stayed with Rocco, echoing in his head long after Clare had fallen asleep in his arms. They were there as he slept, mocking him in his dreams.

They were there as he woke, exhausted and tortured by guilt.

He wasn't who she thought he was.

He wasn't the hero or a knight in shining armor.

And because of the guilt, he couldn't tell her he loved her, not because he didn't love her—my God, she was his world—but because he knew he didn't deserve her. He didn't deserve this perfect little family of his.

For the next week he was in a fog, tormented by the truth and the realization that he'd deceived Clare in the worst sort of way.

Every day he determined to come clean, but then at night, when it was just them, he couldn't bring himself to speak, instead he just wanted her, to be with her, no words, just touch. He let his body tell her what he couldn't—that she was everything to him, and that he'd never loved anyone the way he loved her. He hadn't believed in love at first sight, but from the moment he laid eyes on her, he wanted her, needed her, loved her.

At night he made love to her as if it was their last night, a desperation filling him, as he filled her. He wanted to escape and forget, and as they made love, he could almost forget, but in the morning it all came back.

She didn't know the truth. He should have told her the truth before marrying her.

"What's wrong?" Clare asked at breakfast the next morning. She'd been watching him with a troubled expression for days and he knew she was concerned, but how did he tell her?

What did he say?

"It's nothing," he said, finishing his coffee and rising. He leaned over and kissed her. "I'll see you tonight."

She caught his hand, held it tightly. "You can talk to me, Rocco."

He squeezed her hand in his. "I know."

But as he drove to work he tried to figure out how he'd tell her what weighed so heavily on his conscience. How to tell her something that would hurt her, and potentially tear them apart?

Again that night, after dinner, while lying in bed, Clare stroked his arm lightly, gently. "I can feel your worry," she whispered, her own voice filled with dread. "If there is something you must tell me, please, just tell me. I hate to see you so troubled."

Rocco closed his eyes, his arms closing protectively around her. He didn't want to hurt her. He didn't want to ruin what they had. They were all so happy together, the three of them, it was a good marriage, a deeply satisfying marriage.

But he'd married her under false pretenses.

He'd married her not for Adriano or even for her needs. He'd married her for himself.

Clare eventually slept, but he couldn't, his mind at war with himself. The easy thing would be to let the entire issue go. To pretend he'd been completely honorable in his intentions. To continue on as if he were a good, true, altruistic man. That would be an easy thing, and it would allow them to move forward happily, no bumps, no anger, no drama. But Rocco hated the guilt, and how it made his love feel mean and small.

How it took the beautiful world they'd created and made it dirty. Shameful.

The guilt was eating him alive, and the guilt threatened to destroy the future.

But how did he tell Clare that he'd had ulterior motives in marrying her? How did he say he'd been selfish and determined to make her his? That he'd always wanted her, even when she was engaged to Marius?

He couldn't do that. Only a fool would tell her such a thing. But he must be a fool because he was considering confronting Clare with the truth, all of it. Not because he believed it would make things better, but because he couldn't live with himself like this. He couldn't hide the truth from her. He wanted her. He'd always wanted her. And he couldn't imagine a time when he wouldn't want her, but if there were to be more children, those children should be conceived in love, and truth, and raised in truth, love and honesty. Integrity. Which is how a Cosentino was supposed to be.

Rocco resolved that after dinner, after Adriano was in bed, he'd tell her all of it, and he prayed she would be able to forgive him.

* * *

Clare sat at one end of the leather sofa in the library trying to process what Rocco was saying. She finally put a hand up to stop him. "You're not making sense. Please say that last part again."

Rocco's jaw tightened, his silver gaze shuttered. "Which part?" he gritted.

"The part where you said you struggled with Marius's and my relationship because you had feelings for me." She knotted her hands in her lap, her heart thudding hard. "At least, that's what it sounded like you said."

"That's exactly what I said."

"And you were cold to me because you were trying to remain indifferent to me?"

He nodded once.

Clare's heart hammered and she tried to remain calm, but she was shocked by his admission, shocked that he'd had such strong feelings for her all those years ago. "So the real reason you didn't want Marius to marry me wasn't that you didn't like me," she said after a moment, nails digging into her palms. "It was because you were jealous of him. You wanted me for...yourself."

Rocco's dark head inclined and, horrified, she felt her heart plummet.

What was happening? How could this be real? And if it was true, why was he telling her now? His honesty wasn't to be admired, the truth coming too late. It was all a lie. It was all a big game. She struggled to take it all in, but couldn't, her mind shying away from the facts he'd so calmly laid out, like playing cards onto a table.

"So this was never about Adriano," she whispered, feeling physically ill. "This wasn't about Adriano in any way. It was just your weird possessive need to have me."

Rocco didn't speak and Clare felt her heart break. This couldn't be happening. This couldn't be real.

"I trusted you," she whispered, unable to look at him, unable to let him see how much he'd hurt her, crushing her dreams, smashing her love and faith in him. Their relationship was still so new, but it had been beautiful, and so full of light and warmth, happiness and hope, and now it was all gone.

"I beg your forgiveness. I am determined to earn your trust again," he said.

"No." She rose and, shaking her head, looked at him and then away, too stunned, too much in pain. "No more words. No more anything. I need to be alone. I can't think with you here."

Clare fled to a distant wing of the palazzo, pacing the long sculpture gallery where the walls were lined with framed canvases by centuries of Italy's greatest artists. It was cold in the gallery, but she walked quickly, feeling trapped and panicked. Her pulse was racing and her hands were shaking and she felt on the verge of losing the last shred of control.

She'd come to the gallery because she couldn't go to her bedroom, not when she shared it with Rocco.

She couldn't go anywhere close to the nursery because she couldn't let Ava see her, and certainly not Adriano. She had to protect him from the upheaval. He was so young and so trusting. He needed protection, protection from people—men—who lied and deceived, men who had to win at all costs.

She knew about those men. She'd been raised by one. Her father always had to win, and he'd do whatever it took to have the upper hand.

And to think she'd married one!

Legs trembling, Clare turned at the end of the long gallery and passed pedestals with marble busts, walking between tall marble statues. She was chilled through, and yet fire raged within her, fire burning her heart while on the outside she shivered, teeth chattering.

He'd betrayed her. He'd used Adriano to get to her. Rocco used a child, *her* child—

"Whatever you're doing, whatever you're thinking isn't helping." Rocco's low hard voice came from the end of the gallery. "Stop, please. You're making it worse."

"I'm making this worse?" she choked, anger lashing through her as she spun to face him. "How dare you? How dare you turn this around! My anger isn't about what I did. This is about you, and what you did."

"I didn't want to love you. I didn't want to want you—"

"You were a man, not a prepubescent boy."

"Agreed. *Cara*, I was confounded by my attraction. I am a disciplined man and you were not mine. I shouldn't have been drawn to you. I shouldn't have wanted you, but I did. Don't think I liked feeling that way about you. I tried to create a wall so that I could be detached, but in creating a wall, and creating detachment, Marius took offense. He didn't understand why I couldn't be near you, he couldn't understand why I wasn't more receptive of you, and I couldn't tell him that I was jealous. That I wanted his woman. What kind of brother is so disloyal? I hated myself, and in trying to contain my feelings—"

"You hated me."

"No," Rocco's voice dropped, low, full of pain. "I never hated you. It was Marius I was upset with, Marius for being so lucky to have not just a woman like you, but you."

"That's even worse. Marius was so loving and accepting. He thought you were the greatest man alive. Did he know how you felt about me?"

"No."

"Thank God," she choked. "At least he never knew the truth about you. At least he died thinking you were still the wonderful Rocco Cosentino."

"I loved my brother, and I would have protected him with my life—"

"You're sure you didn't spook the horse that day? Or perhaps you wished him dead?"

"Never." Rocco nearly roared the word. "Never,

ever. I loved him his entire life, and protected him with my life, and his death made me hate myself."

"Good."

Her voice was pitched low, but she knew Rocco heard her. His head lifted and his silver gaze met hers. Clare knew she was being cruel, but in that moment she didn't care. Everything she'd believed was a lie. Everything she'd come to love was false.

Clare sank onto a small upholstered bench, legs no longer able to support her.

"I married you out of love," Rocco said, walking toward her.

She turned her face away from him. "And Adriano? What of him? Or does he not factor in any of this?"

"I love him as my son."

"I don't believe you," she said under her breath, pain and grief washing through her in unrelenting waves.

"I am his father now—"

"No!" She jumped up to stand in front of him, eyes blazing and hands fisted. "You are not his father. Marius was his father. You are…you are…nothing to us."

Rocco gave her the bedroom since she didn't want him there. He slept in the library and spent much of the night watching the fire burn down to a soft red glow. The library grew cold and all was quiet, but there would be no sleeping tonight, not when he felt as if someone had just died. He couldn't lose Clare. She was his world, his heart—

The library door opened and she was there, in a robe, and a blanket over that. "I'm so mad at you," she said from the doorway. "I'm so sad, too. You've ruined everything. It will never be the same."

"Clare, please, come sit down."

"I can't. I can't be near you."

"*Cara*, I know you're hurt—"

"Hurt? Rocco, this isn't hurt. You've destroyed us. You've taken our lives and destroyed us."

"That wasn't my intention."

"What did you expect to happen?" She took a step into the room, her body swallowed by the shadows.

"I don't know," he admitted.

She was shivering as she walked toward him again. "Why tell me in the first place? What did you want from me? Forgiveness? Absolution? But I'm not someone who can absolve you of your sins! I'm not saintly and pious. I'm not going to just shrug and not care, because I'm livid, Rocco. I'm disgusted and filled with so much resentment, and regret. You are not the man I thought I married."

It hurt to breathe. It hurt to hear the pain in her voice. He'd broken her trust and that was a terrible thing to do. "I understand," he said.

"Do you?" she whispered, voice cracking.

He didn't answer immediately. "Yes. I do."

She said nothing, but he heard her exhale. She was crying.

"I'm sorry, Clare."

"You're sorry?" Her voice rose, high and thin. "Is that all you have to say?"

"I don't want to make excuses, Clare. I can't pretend to be the hero anymore. I'm not a hero—"

"So true. You're the antithesis of the hero. You're a pretender. Fake, false, manipulative. You coerced me into marriage. You played the family card, the let's-do-the-best-thing-for-Marius's-son card, knowing I didn't want to marry you, knowing I'd never marry you—"

"You wanted me, too."

"Not like this! Never like this."

Her voice cracked again. She was falling apart, sobbing, broken. He'd done this to her. He'd created this pain and he'd do anything to take it away, make things better. Make things right. "Forgive me, Clare."

"I can't."

"Maybe not now—"

"Never." She was crying so hard she hiccupped. "Did you think I would?"

"I'd hoped."

"Then you're a fool!"

He said nothing and his silence pushed her over the edge.

"Why?" she cried, leaning against a bookcase. "Why couldn't you let me be happy?"

"I wanted you to know the truth—"

"We were doing well. We were happy. Rocco, for God's sake, I was so happy with you. I loved being your wife. I thought finally it's my turn for love and security, and now this? I can't believe you had to do this. I can't believe you felt it necessary to tell me this terrible history between you and your brother."

He didn't know what to say. He wished he had a good answer. He wished he understood himself. Because she was asking all the right questions. But they were questions he didn't have an answer for. Why did he have to do this? Why when she was happy?

And just like that he knew.

Because he didn't trust happiness. And he didn't trust himself.

He didn't feel like a good person and he needed her to love him for who he was, complex and complicated, lonely and confused, hopeful and afraid. He needed her love, and needed her to love him despite the stupid, selfish things he'd done.

Standing there, facing her, he realized that his hope was irrational. One didn't just vomit out one's sins—the crimes committed—and expect forgiveness. As she'd said, she wasn't a priest, she couldn't absolve him. And yet somehow he thought, hoped, she could forgive him. And still love him.

He needed her love.

He needed her.

He needed someone to know him, and accept him, flaws and all. Someone who'd say, *You're not a monster, Rocco.*

But obviously he was. She was horrified and her disgust made him feel such shame.

He didn't want to be a monster. He didn't want to be the bad brother anymore. He loved her, and he loved Adriano, and he wanted to be a husband and father more than he'd ever wanted anything.

In his desire to have complete honesty, he broke her trust. In his desire to build a strong relationship, he'd destroyed the one they'd had.

He'd messed it all up. He destroyed her love. The truth had destroyed the love.

"I am sorry," he said quietly, so quietly because if he'd spoken any louder his voice would crack and his pain would seep out, and he couldn't embarrass himself further. He'd laid himself bare and he'd failed her…and Adriano. Adriano did not deserve any of this, either.

Clare leaned against the bookshelf, head bowed, and the heavy silence filled the dark library, weighting it. After long, painful minutes she exhaled. "I am, too," she whispered, before walking out of the room.

Clare was in a hell of her own making. She'd agreed to marry Rocco for her son's sake. That was why she'd married him. That had been the chief motivating factor. Otherwise, she wouldn't have married. She had no need to marry, but once married to Rocco, she'd discovered how much she liked being married. How much she liked being his wife. How much she craved his touch.

She had enjoyed everything about their marriage—

JANE PORTER                    191

the companionship, the conversations, the meals together, the time spent with Adriano, and of course,
the lovemaking. The lovemaking was unlike anything
she'd known, and it made her feel young and alive,
beautiful and vital. She'd been happy, so happy with
him. But everything she thought was a lie built on
a lie.

He'd married her under false pretenses.

He had not married her with Adriano's best interests at heart. He'd married her to have her, as if she
was a possession to be won. Claimed.

The betrayal was sickening. The betrayal changed
everything. How could she look at Rocco and see
him as she'd seen him before? He wasn't the same
person now. He wasn't honest. He wasn't a man she
could admire, much less a man she trusted around
her child.

There was no way to move forward with Rocco.
She couldn't imagine ever looking at him without
seeing his selfishness. The ugliness. The absolute
lack of morals and character.

There could be no future.

Rocco wasn't the right person. Not for her, and not
for him. He wasn't who she'd thought he was. He'd
deceived them all, but it was over. She was done.

Rocco woke early, but not early enough. Clare and
Adriano were gone. He'd known she'd want him to
leave, or maybe even ask him to leave, but he hadn't
thought it would happen in the middle of the night.

He'd thought there would be more time. He'd thought there might be another conversation. He was wrong, so wrong about so many things.

His staff treated him as they always did—with respect and formality. There was no unnecessary conversation. He was presented with his coffee and his newspaper. He had a second espresso later with a roll. He didn't touch either.

He didn't ask his staff for information about when Clare left, or why no one had alerted him because it served no point. The fact was, she'd gone and they knew. But did they know it was his fault? Did they know he'd brought the destruction on himself?

A brief email arrived in his inbox when he was at work.

I will be initiating a legal separation until we can begin the divorce. You are to stay away from us. I do not wish to hear from you, and you are not to contact me, or Adriano. I have instructed Gio to enforce no communication—no mail, no calls, no appearances. If you ever cared for me, you will respect my wishes. Clare

The weeks passed, and then a month, and another without another word from Clare. There was no communication, not at Christmas, or in the new year.

Christmas in the palazzo was so miserable that he realized he was done with the mausoleum of a place, and done with Rome, too. Not just temporarily, but permanently. He had grown up in this huge, sprawling marble edifice and he'd done his best to make it comfortable for Marius, but there was no reason to try to be comfortable, or happy there any longer. He was tired of taking care of it, tired of being trapped by it.

As he returned to the house from his office it crossed his mind that there was no reason to keep it. He didn't have to. So what if it had been in the family for centuries? So what if he was its custodian? He didn't like being responsible for a place that he didn't enjoy. Which led to another question—what did he enjoy? Where did he enjoy being? Because if Rome wasn't to be his home anymore, where did he want to be?

Where could he go when he didn't feel as if he belonged anywhere anymore?

# CHAPTER NINE

As THE MONTHS PASSED Clare grew even more unhappy. She was miserable. Beyond miserable.

She could barely drag herself from bed to her desk
at her villa. She faked it, of course, for Adriano's
sake, who didn't understand what was happening but
was young enough to believe it was all temporary,
and in his mind Papa Rocco was just "traveling."

But Clare leaned on Ava more than ever, needing
Ava to keep Adriano busy. From her office window
Clare could see them on the lawn playing soccer. Gio
even joined in a game now and then. Clare was glad
Adriano was protected from the pain she was feeling,
because Clare struggled to function. Dressing was
a chore, eating was the most unpleasant activity she
could do. She lived on coffee and now and then a bite
of something, but every time she tried to chew, food
stuck in her throat and it was painful to swallow.

She'd cried so much she despised herself, and
the sadness was all-pervasive. Her body ached, her
chest so tight and heavy that it was as if she'd swal-

lowed an enormous stone. The grief she'd felt when Marius died was one thing, but this was different, this was, this was a pain she had not asked for or needed, a pain that stemmed from betrayal and heart-break. Marius's funeral had brought a terrible closure to their life and relationship, a devastating end to all those dreams they'd shared with each other. But now, Clare felt utterly lost, her heart and body no longer her own because Rocco wasn't dead, he was just somewhere else, and that…that seemed unforgiveable. She didn't want anything bad to happen to him—she did care for him, even if she wished she didn't—but he was too alive in her mind, too present in her heart. If she closed her eyes she could picture Rocco at the lake villa, could see him in his car, could imagine him at work, and in every image he was so alive, while she was here, hurting. Suffering.

She'd grown to hope they'd have a long life together, a good life, one filled with warmth and happiness. She thought she'd finally found happiness again. She thought, she thought… Oh, everything she thought was wrong.

It wasn't fair! None of this was fair. If only she hadn't given him a chance, if only she'd refused his proposal. If only she didn't miss him so much.

Tidying her desk one day she uncovered a creased slip of paper with a scrawl of words:

*I will love you to the end of time. R*

Clare froze, feeling as if she'd been dropped in a volcano, consumed by lava. She flashed back to the weekend following their honeymoon when he'd presented her with the gift of a delicate pink diamond bracelet, and in the bottom of the jeweler's box was this note on a scrap of paper.

*I will love you to the end of time.*

Trembling, Clare crumpled the letter and threw it in the fire, and then sobbed as it burned.

She cried for the future they weren't going to have. She cried for the weeks of happiness she'd known. She cried for Adriano who would never know his family because she was done with Rocco, done with all Cosentinos, done with Italy.

Clare owned a small island in Greece, it was tiny and rocky with a little cove for a boat, and a few gnarled olive trees at the back. She took Adriano there, along with her immediate staff. Adriano had never been to the island and he wasn't sure he wanted to be there. It was still winter, early February and bitterly cold and windy. The stone house felt chilly even with the furnace on, and the wind rattled the old glass windows night and day despite the wood shutters.

Adriano begged to return to the villa and the lawn where he could play soccer. He wanted to go to Roma and see Papa Rocco. He was so angry that Papa Rocco had forgotten them. Clare bit her tongue, holding back the truth. Adriano was too young, he was sweet and bright and full of light and love. He didn't need to know how manipulative men could be.

By mid-March Clare was desperate to return to

Italy, too. She knew why she'd never spent much time on her little Greek island. It was only an oasis in summer, and in the peak of summer it felt too hot.

No, the island was not idyllic and not a good place to recover from a broken heart.

Clare wished she hadn't burned the note Rocco had given her with the bracelet. The note where he said he loved her. She knew she couldn't trust him, but the note was one of the few things with his writing, and she wished she had something of his to keep. Just a memory.

And yet keeping love notes wouldn't help her get over him. Because she wasn't over him yet.

But she would be, eventually. She had to remain firm. His words were pretty, but his idea of love wasn't hers. Love wasn't manipulative, love wasn't dishonest, love didn't deceive.

The wind in April was even stronger than the March wind. The wind blew through the old house, rattling and whistling, and while it wasn't as cold as it had been in February, it was far from cozy and the wind kept knocking out the electricity, and it was one thing to go without internet for a few days, but another to have no power at all.

Easter week they left Greece and returned to their villa in Italy. Adriano was overjoyed, and after arriving at the estate, he rolled on the lawn, and then dashed down the stairs to the beach, running through the waves, the saltwater soaking his rolled-up jeans.

Clare stood on the beach watching her son, a

fist pressed to her mouth, feeling her worlds collide. He looked like his father, but also his uncle, with his dark hair and eyes, and his sturdy athletic little frame. He wasn't a shy child, and he handled change as well as anyone, but he was smart, sweet and so loving.

He hadn't stopped asking for Rocco, either.

But one day he would. It would just take time.

Adriano was sure Rocco would return for his third birthday. Clare tried to discourage Adriano for believing such a thing because there had been no contact, no calls, nothing at all. As an only child with no cousins and no friends, it was hard to have a proper party, but Clare organized for a colorful tent to be set up in the yard, and a pony for pony rides. She hired a magician and a man with lizards and snakes—so many snakes—and she shuddered as the snakes were brought out, one by one, but Adriano wasn't afraid and wanted to handle them. She watched, heart in her mouth, as a boa wrapped around him, coil after coil, and nodded at Gio when she couldn't bear it any longer.

The chef made Adriano's favorite pasta and pizza, and there was cake and gelato for dessert. Clare had gifts for him, his first bike along with a new football. Some of the staff had small gifts, as well. Adriano seemed happy and as Clare tucked him into bed that night he gave her a fierce hug and thanked her for his birthday party.

"You are so welcome, my love," she answered, leaning over to kiss his forehead and then the tip of his nose. "How is it you are three already?"

He nodded somberly. "I know. I'm old now."

She laughed and then tears started to her eyes. She couldn't bear to admit it, but she'd also half expected Rocco to show today. The fact that he didn't come hurt nearly as bad as the day she left him. She knew she'd told him to stay away, but surely he might have come just to wish Adriano happy birthday?

The fact that he hadn't come, the fact that he'd given them up, the fact that he hadn't fought for them spoke volumes.

She'd hoped…needed—no, she couldn't keep wishing. It was over. The past was over. It was time to move forward with the divorce.

She'd held off from filing for divorce for reasons she couldn't explain, but it was time. Rocco had been gone for months. She'd felt numb for months. Where had all the happiness gone? What had happened to all those beautiful dreams?

She kissed Adriano again and then left him snug in his bed. She was fighting tears as she exited his room, and gave Ava a watery smile as she passed her. Clare didn't want to cry. Crying solved nothing.

In her bedroom she lay down on her bed and pressed her pillow to her cheek. Tears streaked down her face and worn out, she let them fall.

Marius's death was a freak accident, but Rocco wasn't dead. Rocco was alive and doing his thing, living his best life in Rome. So why didn't he make an appearance today for Adriano's birthday? Why didn't he call? Why abandon Adriano?

And then the littlest voice whispered inside her head, *Why abandon me?*

For the first time since that terrible day at the palazzo, Clare hated that they weren't raising Adriano together, and wondered why they couldn't raise him together.

Why couldn't they have managed to be mature adults and do what was best for Adriano? It's why they'd married—to take care of him. But they were failing him. They weren't doing their best for him, or by him.

For the first time in months, Clare didn't block out Rocco. She didn't want to pretend he was gone. Dead. He wasn't dead.

She was so tired of feeling heartsick, so tired of the anger and pain, the grief and disbelief. Why couldn't they come together on special occasions and celebrate Adriano's milestones? Why couldn't they try to be good parents...a loving family?

Clare suddenly wanted to speak with him. Worse, she missed him. She missed his scars and his broken parts, his fierceness and his passionate heart. Rocco wasn't perfect, but he loved her...and she wasn't over him, and she didn't know if she could ever forgive him, but at the same time, she couldn't forget him.

It was so confusing, so consuming. She didn't want to love him anymore, but she did. She wanted to let go of the anger and be civil with him, have a civil relationship for Adriano's sake. If it was possible. Could it be possible?

Perhaps seeing Rocco would give her answers. Maybe a conversation would provide some closure, at least romantically. There had been no closure with Marius. One moment he was there, and the next he was gone. But Rocco…she should talk to him and try to come to an understanding which would allow Adriano to be loved by both of them instead of being in the middle. He shouldn't be in the middle.

Clare pushed the notification on her phone, alerting Gio she needed him. It wasn't the panic alert, but the alert requesting his presence.

Gio was at her door in minutes. Clare welcomed him into her living room. "I need your help," she said. "Can you find out something for me?"

"Of course."

"I want you to drive me to the city tomorrow, but I'm not sure if Rocco will be at his office or at his home. Could you find out where he'll be and take me to him, please?"

Gio hesitated. "He's not in Rome. He closed his offices in Rome months ago."

She frowned. "And the house? The palazzo?"

"Apparently he sold it. Close to two months ago."

She dropped onto the edge of her couch. "The Cosentino home?"

"Yes. I heard about it through one of our staff. I checked into the story, wondering about the facts, and it seems they are true. The house was quietly sold to a private investor. Work is being done on the palazzo now. Some think it's to be turned into a luxury hotel."

Clare shuddered. She'd bought private homes that had been turned into resorts, but she'd never taken a private historic home and created a commercial property from it. "I don't understand why he would sell his home. It doesn't make sense. It was one day going to belong to Adriano. He said Adriano was the heir, and he was to inherit."

"I believe, if I am correct, you told him to set you and Adriano free. I believe by selling the Cosentino palazzo he was doing just this—releasing you and Adriano from your ties and responsibilities to the Cosentino family." Gio looked at her and waited, and after a minute had passed and there was only her silence, he excused himself.

Clare heard the door shut behind him, but she couldn't make herself move. She was shocked, and horrified. Rocco had let the palazzo go? He'd left Rome entirely?

What in God's name had Rocco done?

The week dragged by and May turned into June. Clare was tired of work, tired of the long nights, tired of trying to pretend she wasn't missing Rocco, because she was missing him, even more if such a thing was possible.

During the day she could stay busy and distract

herself with calls and meetings, discussing possible acquisitions, and then there was time with Adriano, and that was by far her favorite part of the day. She'd begun to let him stay up a little later just so they had more time together. But of course he eventually went to bed and it was during the long, quiet nights that Clare couldn't escape herself, or her heartache.

Where had Rocco gone? What was he doing now? Did he ever think of her…of them?

One evening, exhausted, she wept into her pillow, the gorgeous pink diamond bracelet clutched tightly in her fist.

It took her a moment to realize Adriano was with her. "Mama, why are you crying?"

Clare sat up quickly, and setting the bracelet on the nightstand scrubbed her face dry. "I'm not," she said, forcing a watery smile. "What are you doing out of bed?"

"I couldn't sleep. I'm hungry."

"Didn't you eat enough dinner?" she asked, holding a hand out to him.

He climbed up onto her bed and settled into the crook of her arm. "I didn't like it. I don't like fish when it's all mushy."

"I didn't think it was mushy," she said, remembering that she'd had dinner at her desk tonight because of a late night meeting with the vineyard staff in California. "But it is a soft fish."

"No more fish."

"Fish is good for us."

"Pizza is good for us," he answered.

She laughed, and kissed his head. "You like other foods besides pizza. Gnocchi. Ravioli. Spaghetti."

"Gelato. I love gelato."

She felt some of the heaviness in her chest ease. "I like gelato, too."

Adriano snuggled against her, his hand finding hers, fingers lacing tightly. For several minutes they just sat together comforting each other. "Mama?"

"Yes, my love?"

"Where's Papa Rocco?"

The pain returned with a vengeance, so sharp it felt like a knife between her ribs. "He's traveling—"

"Still?"

"He works a lot. He owns many businesses and they all need to see him and speak to him."

"Like you have to do?"

"Yes," she answered, "but I don't travel as much. I prefer working from here. That way I can be with you every day."

Adriano thought about this. "He should do that, too. Work here, so he could see us."

She said nothing. What could she say?

"Or does he not want to see us?" he asked, turning to look up at her, shadows in his beautiful brown eyes. "Does he not want us anymore?"

"He will always love you," she said, hoping the answer would appease him.

Adriano fidgeted. "We should go see him. Go to the palazzo. Maybe he forgot about us. Maybe—"

"He's not in Rome anymore."

"No?"

Clare shook her head. "I'm not sure where he is, maybe Argentina, to take care of your father—" she broke off, bit her lip. "The grapes and the house in Mendoza. You have land and beautiful estates waiting for you there, and vineyards and horses. Remember, you are not just Italian, you are also Argentinian."

"And American," he said. "You are American, remember?"

Clare smiled even as her eyes burned, gritty with tears. Her clever, beautiful boy. "How could I forget?"

She'd found him.

Or more correctly, Gio had found him, and Clare had been wrong. Rocco was not in Argentina but in the Caribbean, on his island.

She made arrangements to travel the next day, leaving Adriano with Ava and Gio at the villa, knowing he'd be safe with them.

Clare packed lightly, and slept poorly, ready to go. She didn't know what she'd say to him once she saw him, but figured those words would come. For now, she just needed to get there.

The ten-hour flight felt endless. She struggled to relax, and when she couldn't nap, watched a movie on the plane's individual movie screen and when that and dinner were over, tried to work. She went through paperwork checking numbers and dates, and then did some reading on her laptop, but she couldn't stay focused, the words dancing around on the screen.

Would Rocco be glad to see her?

What would they say to each other?

It turned out to be easy, once she was in front of him. Anger filled her, anger that he'd promised to care for Adriano and then he'd so quickly abandoned him. "You missed Adriano's birthday," Clare said, voice low. "He turned three just a few weeks ago. May fourteenth—"

"I know. I was there. I came to the villa but was turned away."

She looked at him, astonished. "No one said anything to me."

"Your security is very good and very efficient. I'd hoped Gio would speak to you, but apparently your word is law."

She flinched, hating the sound of that, thinking it made her sound like her father, and he was the last person she wanted to be like. "I wish I'd known. He'd wanted to see you. Adriano asked about you all week and then—" she broke off swallowed, terribly remorseful. "He was disappointed, and I tried to make light of it, but I was wrong. It was a mistake. I've always sworn that I would put him first and I haven't put him first. I had married you so he could have a father, but then I pushed you away."

There was only silence and the silence was heavy and uncomfortable. After a long time Rocco spoke,

"But if it is better for him…if Adriano is doing better without me—"

"He's not." Clare swallowed, deeply ashamed. "He has missed you and I thought by now the missing would have eased, that he might have stopped speaking of you so often but it hasn't happened."

She turned and looked across the room, at the place where they had been so happy back in October. The island had been such a lovely getaway for all of them. There had been few distractions, but they hadn't needed distractions. They had been happy just being together. "I've been selfish. Heady. It was one thing for me to tell you to go away, but it was another for me to make that decision so abruptly for Adriano. I'm not sure how to fix it, but I think something has to be done. Perhaps he could come here and see you, spend some time with you—"

"Without you?" Rocco asked.

Her forehead creased, pain splintering through her heart. "I don't know how to make this work. I don't know how to move forward. I don't know how to navigate this next part."

"You don't think you could forgive?"

His voice, those words, made her heart knot and ache. She was creating pain for him, and the fact that she was determined to stay angry at him baffled her. She didn't consider herself an angry person. She didn't like holding grudges. So why was she?

And then she remembered how he'd sold the Cosentino palazzo and had left Rome, and her anger burned again. "I understand you've sold the palazzo. Why?"

He said nothing and she took several steps toward him. "How could you, Rocco? Why would you? It was Adriano's heritage. It was the Cosentino family home. You could have at least discussed it with me not because I wanted it or needed it, but Adriano is the heir."

"How could I discuss anything with you?" he said quietly. "There has been no contact. Anything I've sent to you has been returned. Any call blocked."

She dropped onto a chair, stressed and exhausted and so confused. "Would you have talked to me about it?"

"Of course. You're my wife."

Not, you were my wife, but you are my wife.

Her eyes burned. "Why did you sell it then?"

"I don't think he should have to inherit a place, and be forced to care for it. The palazzo is huge and expensive, it's a constant financial drain, and it traps him to a place, it traps him to a history he might not want. I did this to protect him, to protect his future. Adriano deserves to choose his future. He should be able to have the life he wants, not the life he must inherit. The problem of being an heir, whether it's to a title, an estate or a legacy, is that you are locked into choices made long before you were ever conceived, choices that can be an unbearable burden."

"You found being a Cosentino a burden?"

"When Marius was alive, it wasn't a burden. The

palazzo was expensive, there were always plumbing and electrical issues, there were ongoing repairs, and big gardens require tremendous care. But I didn't mind then because it was for Marius, because we shared a legacy, and we shared the past. Once he was gone…it was an anchor, and not a good one. I was a caretaker for these immense estates, a conservator for wealth that I'd never spend, and there was no purpose for it—"

"Adriano."

"I didn't know he existed then. I didn't realize there was another generation."

"But you do now, and you've sold the Cosentino palazzo!"

"One's life shouldn't be spent caring for things." He hesitated before adding, "It should be spent caring for people."

His words made her heart ache. She had never been included in her father's circle, she knew little about the people—or things—important to him.

For her, her legacy would be her son, and yes, Rocco was right. Adriano should have freedom to choose his path without being burdened with the relics of a past long gone.

Rocco had done Adriano a favor. She just hadn't understood it at the time.

"What if he should want it in the future?" she asked. "What if he should want that responsibility?"

"Then he will have an opportunity to have it back. The palazzo isn't exactly sold. It's only been leased, albeit, a twenty-year lease to the Italian government. They plan to use it as a museum to house art collections by Italy's twentieth-century artists. The gardens will be open to the public as well, so nothing will be destroyed, everything will be taken care of so should Adriano choose, at the age of twenty-three, to keep his home, the palazzo will be his. And should he want to sell it to the government, they have indicated they would like to own it. But it's up to him. The palazzo is his, held in the Cosentino trust, of which he is the beneficiary."

She didn't know what to say. She hadn't expected any of this. "So you didn't sell his birthright."

"It's not mine to dispose of. He is the future, but that means he chooses his future."

She studied his face, seeing the fatigue there. "You never had that choice, did you?"

He shrugged. "He is Marius's son. But I love him as if he were my own."

Clare blinked back tears, aware that for a time, Adriano was his. She rose, and paced, running a hand across her face, drying her eyes. "I've been so angry with you," she said, pacing back toward him, "for months now. I'm tired of it. I'm tired of feeling this way about someone I once loved."

She saw how he flinched at that and she hated that her words hurt him. She hadn't meant to inflict more pain now. It was time for change. Clare was tired of being angry, tired of grieving; life was too short for all this unhappiness.

"How are you?" she asked him. "Really?"

"Now that you are here, I am better," he answered. "And you? How are you, *cara*?"

She searched his lovely silver eyes so full of sorrow and shadows. "I am better," she whispered, "now that I am here."

"You haven't changed," he said after a moment, lips quirked. "You wouldn't come because you needed me, but you've come because Adriano did."

Clare bit into her lower lip, struggling with her answer. "We both need you," she said unsteadily. "And we both miss you."

Her eyes began to fill with tears and Rocco drew her down onto the white couch, and wrapped his arm around her, holding her close to his chest, and for a moment Clare was afraid to breathe, afraid to move in case this was a dream, but no, she could hear the steady beating of his heart, and the warmth of his skin, and the hard muscle of his chest.

This was real. He was real.

Gradually she relaxed, his warmth soothing her, his arm holding her secure and she wasn't going to think, or let her brain take over. For now, she would just savor being here with him.

It had been so long since she'd felt like things might be okay, and while she didn't know the future, in this moment, right now, in Rocco's arms, her cheek above his heart, she felt peace. She felt as if she was home. Rocco was home.

Her eyes stung and she blinked hard to hold in the emotion.

Love, she loved him, and it had been so hard to be away from him. And it came to her—how did one forgive? You forgave because you loved.

You forgave because you wanted more.

Clare desperately wanted more, not less. She desperately wanted to feel like she belonged somewhere and with someone. Rocco would always be home. Why had she taken so long to see it? Believe it?

Rocco kissed the top of her head. "Don't cry." His voice was low, husky, comforting.

She felt like Adriano when he came to her room late at night, unable to sleep, wanting to feel safe. Everyone needed love, everyone craved family and security. Everyone needed second chances and hope. Good God, she needed hope. The tears she'd been struggling to hold back fell.

"I don't want to lose you, too." Clare said thickly, finding it so hard to talk and breathe while crying. "I don't understand any of this, but I know we should at least talk. Try to have a conversation."

"I agree." He pulled her onto his lap so that both arms could hold her more firmly. "But I think we should have a conversation later when you're done with the tears. So cry now, and I promise you, we'll talk when you're ready."

They did talk later. They talked for hours; they talked and went for a walk, then talked again and kissed.

The kiss had surprised him because she'd been the one to reach out to him. She'd caught his face in her hands and studied it, looking deep into his eyes before whispering, "I do love you. And if you still love me, is there a future for us?"

"Yes." He kissed her, once and then again. "You are my future. You, and Adriano, are everything to me. But since you are here, let me show you just how much I've missed you and want you."

"I think that's a very good idea," she murmured, shivering as his lips brushed across her neck, and then lower, light kisses along her collarbone and then lower still.

He did show her how much he loved her. He showed her all night long.

Love is patient.

And true love forgives.

# EPILOGUE

THE BEST MONTHS to visit the Caribbean were in the fall, between October and December, and as Rocco wanted the children to grow up with an American Thanksgiving, they began to go to their island late November, where they'd remain until mid-December, when they'd return to the seaside villa outside Rome.

Adriano was always thrilled to return to the island. Fortunately, so were his younger brothers and sister as each arrived, growing from infants to toddlers and from toddlers to proper playmates. Adriano was always very careful to teach them about the dangers of the ocean, as well as all the different fountains and pools.

One early December when Adriano was nine years old, Clare emerged from the house with arms filled with towels as they were all going to the pool for a swim. The children were waiting for her on the patio, but she could hear Adriano speaking quite sternly to his five-year-old brother, four-year-old sis-

ter and the two-year-old baby, Jaco, whom Adriano
was holding by the hand.

"See this," Adriano said gesturing to the infin-
ity pool that overlooked the ocean, "this is dangerous. You can drown, Jaco. If you fell in you'd die.
So never, *ever* go near the pool or touch the water
unless Mama and Papa are with you."

Hidden by the shadow of a potted tree, Clare
bit her lip, fighting her smile, proud of her very responsible oldest son. Adriano was more like Rocco
than any of the younger ones. Five-year-old Marcus
was the wild one, constantly on the go. Four-year-
old Daniela was a little timid but terribly loyal and
sweet. While two-year-old Jaco was in awe of the
older siblings.

Adriano wasn't just a good brother, but a good
son, always aware of the dangers, and determined
to protect his family. He didn't like risk. He thought
carefully about potential problems, and never believed that one nanny should watch all the kids because something could still happen.

"But I can swim," Marcus said exasperated, an-
noyed that Adriano was once again giving a lecture.
"I swim even better than you, Adriano."

Daniela made a gasping sound. "Adriano is a great
swimmer. He is the best, Marcus, and he's the oldest."

Rocco emerged then from the house, joining Clare
in the shadows of the tree. He saw her watching the

children, and whispered, "Who are we spying on, and why?"

She looked up at him, smiling into his eyes, thinking he was far more gorgeous now than when they'd married. "We're spying on the children as Adriano is teaching about the dangers of the ocean…as well as all the pools and fountains."

Rocco arched a brow. "Again?"

She smothered a laugh. "But this time there's Jaco, and he must be taught, too. Adriano takes his job as the big brother very seriously."

"Very seriously," Rocco agreed, wrapping his arms around Clare, and holding her against him. "We're lucky."

"So lucky," she agreed, sighing softly as he kissed the side of her neck, and sighing again as his hands caressed the length of her before sliding up to cup her breasts. "This is how we end up pregnant," she said, a little breathless. "Don't you think four little Cosentinos might be enough?"

"Probably," he murmured, one of his hands slipping beneath her bikini top, palming her bare breast and the pert nipple. "But it's good to practice, just in case."

She was melting, just as she always did, and as his teeth scraped the side of her neck, Clare pressed her bottom against his hard body, loving him, loving the feel of him, loving the life they'd made together.

"We can practice tonight," she said, trying very hard to be quiet when he was setting her body on fire.

"Or maybe during nap time?"

"Or maybe both if you're good."

He pinched her nipple just hard enough for her to whimper and wiggle against him. "Oh, *cara*, my love, I am always good."

She laughed even as she sighed. "So true."

\* \* \* \* \*

### #4165 A NINE-MONTH DEAL WITH HER HUSBAND
*Hot Winter Escapes*
### by Joss Wood
Millie Piper's on-paper marriage to CEO Benedikt Jónsson gave her ownership over her life and her billion-dollar inheritance. Now Millie wants a baby, so it's only right that she asks Ben for a divorce first. She doesn't expect her shocking attraction to her convenient husband! Dare she propose that *Ben* father her child?

### #4166 SNOWBOUND WITH THE IRRESISTIBLE SICILIAN
*Hot Winter Escapes*
### by Maya Blake
Shy Giada Parker can't believe she agreed to take her überconfident twin's place in securing work with ruthless Alessio Montaldi. Until a blizzard strands her in Alessio's opulent Swiss chalet and steeling her body against his magnetic gaze becomes Giada's hardest challenge yet!

### #4167 UNDOING HIS INNOCENT ENEMY
*Hot Winter Escapes*
### by Heidi Rice
Wildlife photographer Çara prizes her independence as the only way to avoid risky emotional entanglements. Until a storm traps her in reclusive billionaire Logan's luxurious lodge, and there's nowhere to hide from their sexual tension! Logan's everything Cara shouldn't want but he's all she craves...

### #4168 IN BED WITH HER BILLIONAIRE BODYGUARD
*Hot Winter Escapes*
### by Pippa Roscoe
Visiting an Austrian ski resort is the first step in Hope Harcourt's plan to take back her family's luxury empire. Having the gorgeous security magnate Luca Calvino follow her every move, protecting her from her unscrupulous rivals, isn't! Especially when their forbidden relationship begins to cross a line...

**YOU CAN FIND MORE INFORMATION ON UPCOMING HARLEQUIN TITLES, FREE EXCERPTS AND MORE AT HARLEQUIN.COM.**

HPCNMRB1123

# Get 3 FREE REWARDS!

## We'll send you 2 FREE Books plus a FREE Mystery Gift.

PRESENTS
His Innocent for
One Spanish Night
CAROL MARINELLI

PRESENTS
Bound by the
Italian's "I Do"
MICHELLE SMART

FREE
Value Over
$20

Both the **Harlequin® Desire** and **Harlequin Presents®** series feature compelling novels filled with passion, sensuality and intriguing scandals.

# HARLEQUIN
## PLUS

Try the best multimedia subscription service for romance readers like you!

---

## Read, Watch and Play.

Experience the easiest way to get the romance content you crave.

Start your **FREE TRIAL** at
www.harlequinplus.com/freetrial.